"I'm telling you, I was murdered."

Ruthie's voice escalated. She pointed her bony finger at me. "You are going to help me get to the other side by figuring out who killed me."

"Other side?"

"Great beyond. The light. The big guy in the sky." Ruthie looked up to the ceiling, and then back to me. "I can't cross over until I can rest eternal. And that means catching my killer."

"Killer?" The sound of it made me more worried than scared. Was there really a killer on the loose in Sleepy Hollow? Or was there just one person out to get Ruthie Sue Payne and why?

"Fine." I bit my lip. I couldn't believe what I was about to say. I paused and thought one more second before I spoke. "If trying to find out *who killed you* will get you out of here and not let everyone think I have a case of the 'Funeral Trauma' I'll do it."

I reached over and picked up one of Ruthie's memorial cards and the pen from the visitor log. "Tell me what you remember."

TONYA KAPPES

A GHOSTLY UNDERTAKING

A GHOSTLY SOUTHERN MYSTERY

WITNESS

An Imprint of HarperCollinsPublishers

This book was originally published in 2013 in e-book format, in a slightly altered version.

WITNESS

An Imprint of HarperCollins*Publishers*
195 Broadway
New York, New York 10007

Copyright © 2013, 2015 by Tonya Kappes
Excerpt from *A Ghostly Grave* copyright © 2015 by Tonya Kappes
ISBN 978-0-06-237464-6
www.witnessimpulse.com

First Witness mass market printing: March 2015

HarperCollins ® is a registered trademark of HarperCollins Publishers.

Printed in the United States of America

10 9 8 7 6 5 4 3 2 1

A
GHOSTLY
UNDERTAKING

Chapter 1

Another day. Another funeral. Another ghost.

Great. As if people didn't think I was freaky enough. But, truthfully, this was becoming a common occurrence for me as the director of Eternal Slumber Funeral Home.

Well, the funeral thing was common.

The ghost thing . . . that was new, making Sleepy Hollow anything *but* sleepy.

"What is *she* doing here?" A ghostly Ruthie Sue Payne stood next to me in the back of her own funeral, looking at the long line of Sleepy Hollow's residents that had come to pay tribute to her life. "I couldn't stand her while I was living, much less dead."

Ruthie, the local innkeeper, busybody and my

granny's arch-nemesis, had died two days ago after a fall down the stairs of her inn.

I hummed along to the tune of "Blessed Assurance," which was piping through the sound system, to try and drown out Ruthie's voice as I picked at baby's breath in the pure white blossom funeral spray sitting on the marble-top pedestal table next to the casket. The more she talked, the louder I hummed and rearranged the flowers, gaining stares and whispers of the mourners in the viewing room.

I was getting used to those stares.

"No matter how much you ignore me, I know you can hear and see me." Ruthie rested her head on my shoulder, causing me to nearly jump out of my skin. "If I'd known you were a light seeker, I probably would've been a little nicer to you while I was living."

I doubted that. Ruthie Sue Payne hadn't been the nicest lady in Sleepy Hollow, Kentucky. True to her name, she was a pain. Ruthie had been the president and CEO of the gossip mill. It didn't matter if the gossip was true or not, she told it.

Plus, she didn't care much for my family. Especially not after my granny married Ruthie's ex-husband, Earl. And *especially* not after Earl died and left Granny his half of the inn he and Ruthie had owned together . . . the inn where Granny and Ruthie both lived. The inn where Ruthie had died.

I glared at her. Well, technically I glared at Pastor Brown, because he was standing next to me and he obviously couldn't see Ruthie standing between us. Honestly, I wasn't sure there was a ghost between us, either. It had been suggested that the visions I had of dead people were hallucinations . . .

I kept telling myself that I was hallucinating, because it seemed a lot better than the alternative—I could see ghosts, talk to ghosts, be touched by ghosts.

"Are you okay, Emma Lee?" Pastor Brown laid a hand on my forearm. The sleeve on his brown pin-striped suit coat was a little too small, hitting above his wrist bone, exposing a tarnished metal watch. His razor-sharp blue eyes made his coal-black greasy comb-over stand out.

"Yes." I lied. "I'm fine." Fine as a girl who was having a ghostly hallucination could be.

"Are you sure?" Pastor Brown wasn't the only one concerned. The entire town of Sleepy Hollow had been worried about my well-being since my run-in with Santa Claus.

No, the spirit of Santa Claus hadn't visited me. *Yet*. Three months ago, a plastic Santa had done me in.

It was the darndest thing, a silly accident.

I abandoned the flower arrangement and smoothed a wrinkle in the thick velvet drapes, remembering that fateful day. The sun had been out, melting away the last of the Christmas snow. I'd decided to walk over to Artie's Meats and Deli, over on Main Street, a block away from the funeral home, to grab a bite for lunch since they had the best homemade chili this side of the Mississippi. I'd just opened the door when the snow and ice around the plastic Santa Claus Artie had put on the roof of the deli gave way, sending the five-foot jolly man crashing down on my head, knocking me out.

Flat out.

I knew I was on my way to meet my maker when Chicken Teater showed up at my hospital bedside. I had put Chicken Teater in the ground two years ago. But there he was, telling me all sorts of crazy things that I didn't understand. He blabbed on and on about guns, murders and all sorts of dealings I wanted to know nothing about.

It wasn't until my older sister and business partner, Charlotte Rae Raines, walked right through Chicken Teater's body, demanding that the doctor do something for my hallucinations, that I realized I wasn't dead after all.

I had been *hallucinating*. That's all. Hallucinating.

Doc Clyde said I had a case of the "Funeral Trauma" from working with the dead too long.

Too long? At twenty-eight, I had been an undertaker for only three years. I had been around the funeral home my whole life. It was the family business, currently owned by my granny, but run by my sister and me.

Some family business.

Ruthie tugged my sleeve, bringing me out of my memories. "And her!" she said, pointing across the room. Every single one of Ruthie's fingers was filled up to its knuckles with rings. She had been very specific in her funeral "pre-need" arrangements, and had diagramed where she wanted every single piece of jewelry placed on her during her viewing. The jewelry jangled as she wagged a finger at Sleepy Hollow's mayor, Anna Grace May. "I've been trying to get an appointment to see her for two weeks and she couldn't make time for me. Hmmph."

Doc Clyde had never been able to explain the touching thing. If Ruthie *was* a hallucination, how could she touch me? I rubbed my arm, trying to erase the feeling, and watched as everyone in the room turned their heads toward Mayor May.

Ruthie crossed her arms, lowered her brow and

snarled. "Must be an election year, her showing up here like this."

"She's pretty busy," I whispered.

Mayor May sashayed her way up to see old Ruthie laid out, shaking hands along the way as if she were the president of the United States about to deliver the State of the Union speech. Her long, straight auburn hair was neatly tucked behind each ear, and her tight pencil skirt showed off her curvy body in just the right places. Her perfect white teeth glistened in the dull funeral-home setting.

If she wasn't close enough to shake your hand, the mayor did her standard wink and wave. I swear that was how she got elected. Mayor May was the first Sleepy Hollow official to ever get elected to office without being born and bred here. She was a quick talker and good with the old people, who made up the majority of the population. She didn't know the history of all the familial generations—how my grandfather had built Eternal Slumber with his own hands or how Sleepy Hollow had been a big coal town back in the day—which made her a bit of an outsider. Still, she was a good mayor and everyone seemed to like her.

All the men in the room eyed Mayor May's wiggle as she made her way down the center aisle of the viewing room. A few smacks could be heard from the women punching their husbands in the arm to stop them from gawking.

Ruthie said, "I know, especially now with that new development happening in town. It's why I wanted to talk to her."

New development? This was the first time I had heard anything about a new development. There hadn't been anything new in Sleepy Hollow in . . . a long time.

We could certainly use a little developing, but it would come at the risk of disturbing Sleepy Hollow's main income. The town was a top destination in Kentucky because of our many caves and caverns. Any digging could wreak havoc with what was going on underground.

Before I could ask Ruthie for more information, she said, "It's about time *they* got here."

In the vestibule, all the blue-haired ladies from the Auxiliary Club (Ruthie's only friends) stood side by side with their pocketbooks hooked in the crooks of their elbows. They were taking their sweet time signing the guest book.

The guest book was to be given to the next of

kin, whom I still hadn't had any luck finding. As a matter of fact, I didn't have any family members listed in my files for Ruthie.

Ruthie walked over to her friends, eyeing them as they talked about her. She looked like she was chomping at the bit to join in the gossip, but put her hand up to her mouth. The corners of her eyes turned down, and a tear balanced on the edge of her eyelid as if she realized her fate had truly been sealed.

A flash of movement caught my eye, and I nearly groaned as I spotted my sister Charlotte Rae snaking through the crowd, her fiery gaze leveled on me. I tried to sidestep around Pastor Brown but was quickly jerked to a stop when she called after me.

"Did I just see you over here talking to yourself, Emma Lee?" She gave me a death stare that might just put me next to old Ruthie in her casket.

"Me? No." I laughed. When it came to Charlotte Rae, denial was my best defense.

My sister stood much taller than me. Her sparkly green eyes, long red hair, and girl-next-door look made families feel comfortable discussing their loved one's final resting needs with her. That was why she ran the sales side of our business, while I covered almost everything else.

Details. That was my specialty. I couldn't help but notice Charlotte Rae's pink nails were a perfect match to her pink blouse. She was perfectly beautiful.

Not that I was unattractive, but my brown hair was definitely dull if I didn't get highlights, which reminded me that I needed to make an appointment at the hair salon. My hazel eyes didn't twinkle like Charlotte Rae's. Nor did my legs climb to the sky like Charlotte's. She was blessed with Grandpa Raines's family genes of long and lean, while I took after Granny's side of the family—average.

Charlotte Rae leaned over and whispered, "Seriously, are you seeing something?"

I shook my head. There was no way I was going to spill the beans about seeing Ruthie. Truth be told, I'd been positive that seeing Chicken Teater while I was in the hospital *had* been a figment of my imagination . . . until I was called to pick up Ruthie's dead body from the Sleepy Hollow Inn and Antiques, Sleepy Hollow's one and only motel.

When she started talking to me, there was no denying the truth.

I wasn't hallucinating.

I could see ghosts.

I hadn't quite figured out what to do with this newfound talent of mine, and didn't really want to discuss it with anyone until I did. Especially Charlotte. If she suspected what was going on, she'd have Doc Clyde give me one of those little pills that he said cured the "Funeral Trauma," but only made me sleepy and groggy.

Charlotte Rae leaned over and fussed at me through her gritted teeth. "If you are seeing something or *someone*, you better keep your mouth shut."

That was one thing Charlotte Rae was good at. She could keep a smile on her face and stab you in the back at the same time. She went on. "You've already lost Blue Goose Moore and Shelby Parks to Burns Funeral Home because they didn't want the 'Funeral Trauma' to rub off on them."

My lips were as tight as bark on a tree about seeing or hearing Ruthie. In fact, I didn't understand enough of it myself to speak of it.

I was saved from more denials as the Auxiliary women filed into the viewing room one by one. I jumped at the chance to make them feel welcome—and leave my sister behind. "Right this way, ladies." I gestured down the center aisle for the Auxiliary women to make their way to the casket.

One lady shook her head. "I can't believe she fell down the inn's steps. She was always so good on her feet. So sad."

"It could happen to any of us," another blue-haired lady rattled off as she consoled her friend.

"Yes, it's a sad day," I murmured and followed them up to the front of the room, stopping a few times on the way so they could say hi to some of the townsfolk they recognized.

"Fall?" Ruthie leaned against her casket as the ladies paid their respects. "What does she mean 'fall'?" Ruthie begged to know. Frantically, she looked at me and back at the lady.

I ignored her, because answering would really set town tongues to wagging, and adjusted the arrangement of roses that lay across the mahogany casket. The smell of the flowers made my stomach curl. There was a certain odor to a roomful of floral arrangements that didn't sit well with me. Even as a child, I never liked the scent.

Ruthie, however, was not going to be ignored.

"Emma Lee Raines, I know you can hear me. You listen to me." There was a desperate plea in her voice. "I didn't fall."

Okay, *that* got my attention. I needed to hear this. I gave a sharp nod of my chin, motioning for her to follow me.

Pulling my hands out of the rose arrangement, I smoothed down the front of my skirt and started to walk back down the aisle toward the entrance of the viewing room.

We'd barely made into the vestibule before Ruthie was right in my face. "Emma Lee, I did *not* fall down those stairs. Someone pushed me. Don't you understand? I was murdered!"

Chapter 2

Murdered? There had never been a murder in Sleepy Hollow—that I knew of.

I hadn't known what to say to Ruthie, and needed time to think things through, so I punched open the swinging door leading to the employee gathering space and headed for my office.

If I didn't think I'd be interrupted, I'd pull the shades and lie down on one of the couches to rest. That was too much to ask. Even though the employees hung out there during their breaks, during funerals the guests would also go back there to talk or visit, away from the body. Today was no different.

The couches were lined with the good citizens of Sleepy Hollow, gossiping about the abrupt death of one of Sleepy Hollow's staple residents: Ruthie.

I overheard a few of them saying they were in shock and didn't realize she was so unstable.

They are shocked? I passed by them. I was shocked.

Once inside my office, I planted my back against the door. In the darkness, my heavy breathing bounced off the wood-paneled walls, breaking the stillness in the room.

Silence. The ghost of Ruthie Sue Payne was nowhere to be seen—she hadn't followed me here. She'd dropped her little bombshell and skedaddled.

"Murdered." I closed my eyes. Was it possible?

Of course one of my staff would have noticed some sign of that while they were prepping Ruthie's body. But a niggling doubt had appeared. I gave myself a good shake. "Emma Lee Raines, take ahold of yourself."

Slipping off my high heels, I ran my hands along the wall and walked into the bathroom, flipping on the light switch. The cold tile shocked my feet, making me jump a little.

I turned the hot water faucet on. The old pipes groaned as I held my hand under the stream, waiting, waiting. Tonight, the sound sent chills up my spine . . . and the cold stream felt like ice. My nerves were definitely on edge.

I looked in the mirror at the dark circles under my eyes.

"You *can* get control of your life." I tapped the bags under my eyes. I once heard the power of positive affirmation could do wonders for your psyche. I was banking on that.

At last the water ran warm. Using cupped hands, I splashed warm water on my face until I felt like a drowned rat.

I grabbed the towel, dabbed the water off my face and eyed my reflection. My dull brown hair—not to mention the dripping mascara half-way down my cheek from the water—made me look like a boring funeral girl who just might have a case of the crazies.

"Better." *Positive affirmation.* I smiled as I opened the medicine cabinet.

Ruthie's voice came from behind me. "What-ever you're looking for, you might want to take two. You're looking a little ghostly yourself. I'm sorry if I knocked you for a loop with my murder news, but I need your help, Emma Lee."

The towel dropped to my feet as my mouth

dropped open, too. My stomach hit my toes and bounced up, lodging in my throat. I tried to speak, but couldn't.

Surely this wasn't Ruthie. Ruthie Sue Payne would never be caught in hot pink pajamas, kitty-cat slippers and her hair tucked in a night cap. Fingers full of rings, maybe, but *this*?

Ruthie eyed me. "What? Ghost got your tongue?"

"You *are* a ghost?" I squeezed my eyes shut and slowly opened them. I was seeing things. But she was still there, hot pink pj's and all. I dragged my finger up and down in the air. "Ruthie would never be caught dead, no pun intended, in those."

"If I was sleeping, I would," she said. She flung her foot out to the side; the kitty-slipper eyes jingled along with the jewels on her hands as she did spirit fingers. "I'm a ghost and someone killed me. You are seeing me. You are the only one who sees me."

"Doc Clyde said something about hallucinations. And I think I might be having one right this moment." I bit my lip and paced back and forth, wondering if I should yell for Charlotte.

"He's a moron."

Since Ruthie was so chatty, I was about to pepper her with questions. Lots of hows and whys. *How was I able to see her? Why was she talking to me? And why did she think she'd been murdered?* But before I could, I heard a tap on my office door, then the room flooded with light. "Emma Lee?"

Ruthie's eyes widened and she put her finger up to her mouth, "Shh . . ."

"I'm here!" I screamed, hoping that it would scare the hallucination or Ruthie's ghost off. It didn't matter which one left, as long as it left.

I had never been so relieved to see Charlotte Rae poke her pretty little head into my bathroom. "Emma Lee, what are you doing in here? What happened to your makeup? Are you okay?"

She took her hand and rubbed it across my cheek, wiping off smudged makeup. For a second there, I thought she was going to spit on a napkin and go in for another rub, so I dodged to the side.

"What are you looking at?" Charlotte glanced over her shoulder. Her perfectly coifed red hair didn't move.

"Nothing." I smiled, brushing down the front of my skirt as if there was some stray lint. "There was a lull in the visitation, so I wanted to come freshen up my makeup."

I lied . . . for the second time tonight.

Charlotte Rae took the opportunity to look in the mirror. She grabbed the hand towel and rubbed the jeweled buttons on her jacket, making them sparkle even more. "Hurry up. The visitation is almost over. You need to go over all the final touches for the burial before tomorrow."

Tomorrow! Would Ruthie be gone tomorrow? I'd been so sure that Ruthie was going to be like Chicken Teater: here one minute and gone the next. Once Ruthie's body was in the ground, would she be gone . . . forever?

I had no idea—but maybe Ruthie knew. "I'll be right out—I just need a few more minutes."

Charlotte Rae grabbed my arm. "No, now. The place is packed and I need your help."

As she grabbed my arm and dragged me along, I grabbed my high heels, and actually hoped that Ruthie would stick around a while longer so I could ask those questions. Murdered. It didn't seem possible.

Back in the viewing room, the place buzzed with Sleepy Hollow residents. The first and last hours of a funeral visitation were the busiest. People believed that if you got there early, you got out early. Or if you got there late, you had to leave by closing time. Let's face it, who wants to be face-to-face with a corpse for any length of time?

Besides my crazy family, that is.

As I made my way back to Ruthie's casket, I

overheard a conversation between two men sitting in one of the rows. I paused for a moment to hear exactly what they thought about her sudden death.

One gentleman hung his head and stared at his fingers, which were folded in his lap. He said, "I knew those stairs were too steep."

The other man, who couldn't take his eyes off of Ruthie's casket, added, "That inn needs to be bulldozed. It's dangerous and old."

"You never know." The first man shook his head. "Ruthie was getting up in age and maybe she wasn't as with it as we thought."

"She wasn't crazy." The second gentleman was offended.

"Not crazy," he corrected himself. "We aren't as spry as we use to be."

The other man nodded in agreement. His eyes deepened along with his lines.

Leaning up against her casket, Ruthie fiddled with the jewels on her fingers. "Half of these people are only here to be nosy. Most of them hated me, you know. And I bet my murderer is in this very room. Who could it be . . . ? Hmm. I suppose there's no lack of suspects. Someone came up behind me and shoved me down those stairs. Could be just about anyone, including your granny, you know. She'd been itching to push me down those steps for years."

That was true. Granny hated Ruthie. But Granny wasn't the type to murder someone and not take blame for it. She'd be going around town bragging about what she'd done.

"You're going to have your hands full trying to figure it out," Ruthie added.

I smiled and nodded at all the people walking past and gawking at Ruthie's body, wondering if they could tell that I was listening to a ghost rant. But even though I couldn't openly speak to Ruthie here and now, she did have me thinking . . . about who could have killed her.

Even if Ruthie was right and all of these people were here to see what was going on, they all did seem to have some sadness about them. No one said a foul word about her.

"It's so good of you to stand up here to greet everyone." One of the local elderly women patted my arm when she walked by.

It really wasn't my place to stand by the casket, it was the job of the next of kin or any sort of family. Unfortunately, Ruthie didn't have any next of kin listed on her pre-arrangement form, nor could I find any.

I'm all she had.

I glanced over at the grandfather clock that stood in the corner. The brass weights and pendulum were polished to a high shine. Only twenty more minutes to go before everyone left and I could talk to Ruthie without fear of being overheard.

Charlotte walked up and nudged me. "I can't help but feel a little victorious that Ruthie is lying in the same spot from where she stole Earl." There was a little pleasure in her voice. "That's some kind of karma."

I glanced over at Charlotte and couldn't help but smile. Old Ruthie had her hand up to her nose and was wiggling her fingers with her tongue stuck out, like a six-year-old. Ruthie had never been this funny when she was living.

Five years ago, Earl Way Payne, Ruthie's deceased ex-husband, had lain in the exact same spot as Ruthie . . . until Ruthie stole him.

On the day of his funeral, Earl Way's will was read, leaving Granny his half of the Inn.

Apparently, Earl Way hadn't changed his "pre-need" funeral arrangements when he married my granny and hadn't let her know what his plans were. So, Granny had Earl Way laid out in this very viewing room as if he were the king of England, with a room full of Sleepy Hollow residents here paying their respects, when O'Dell Burns marched in, rolling a casket cot, with Ruthie right behind him.

"Pick him up," Ruthie had demanded, pointing back and forth from Earl Way's body to the basic wooden box O'Dell had wheeled in. "Go on, put him in."

I had never seen Granny speechless, but she was that day. O'Dell picked up Earl Way's body and plopped him into that cheap pine box.

Granny had stood at the front door with her arms crossed as O'Dell barreled out of the viewing room with Earl hopping and bopping and Ruthie scurrying alongside.

And no one could do a darned thing about it, because old Earl hadn't changed the orders to make Granny in charge of his eternal rest. That duty had been left to Ruthie, and she was determined to see it out. Her way.

That was the moment when Granny decided to move into Earl's side of the Sleepy Hollow Inn and make Ruthie's life miserable.

A hymnal played through the intercom, bringing me back to reality, or the reality that I had come to know.

Some of the people had filtered out into the employee gathering space, while others mingled in the hallway just outside of the vestibule.

" 'Low in the Valley?' " Ruthie cried out. "I know that song wasn't in my pre-need packet. I couldn't stand that song living, let alone dead!"

We both looked at Charlotte. She had a smug smile on her face.

"Charlotte Rae Raines," I gasped at my sister. " 'Low in the Valley' was not in Ruthie's 'pre-need' arrangements."

Charlotte shrugged her shoulders. "Sometimes the music gets mixed up."

This was no mix-up. Charlotte was making a dig at Ruthie on Granny's behalf.

Ruthie was spitting mad. She vanished into thin air, which made me feel a little bit better. I was too busy watching her instead of doing my job.

I refilled the memorial cards and made sure there were plenty of mints in the glass bowls as I walked around and greeted the mourners.

There were a few people here I didn't recognize. Casually I walked over to the chairs and sat diagonally behind Mayor May and a gentleman I didn't know.

"Is this little hiccup going to hinder our little deal?" the man asked. He was shaped like a bull and looked like a sausage in a gray pin-striped suit. His beefy fingers scratched his nose before rubbing the back of his football player's neck, like he was trying to work out the stress of the conversation they were having.

Mayor May smiled, batting her long eyelashes. Her teeth were as white as the strand of pearls around her neck. "I'll take the proposal to the town council."

"You better figure out who the next of kin is," the man hinted a threat. "We'll need approval."

I could only assume he was talking about Ruthie's next of kin. No one in town seemed to know anything about her. When I was filing all the paperwork for her arrangements, the next of kin was supposed to sign off on it. I went to the mayor and the local sheriff, Jack Henry Ross, to see if they knew anything. Neither of them had a clue. There wasn't a will to be found, either. Nothing.

Per the funeral director code of ethics, I had to do everything in my power to find Ruthie Sue Payne's next of kin.

Reaching into my suit pocket, I grabbed my cell phone and tapped the calendar application. The town council meeting was coming up and I wanted to make sure I didn't miss it—the proposal Mayor May was talking about had me intrigued.

Ruthie appeared out of nowhere . . . again.

This time, there was something wrong with Ruthie, and it was more than just her listening to "Low in the Valley." She darted back, forth, and leaned over her dead body.

"Where is my brooch?" She yelled so loud, I put my hands over my ears. The woman sitting next to me oddly smiled and casually got up as if the "Funeral Trauma" was like bedbugs.

Contagious.

"In my arrangements, I specifically said that I wanted my spider diamond brooch on my left side." She pointed to her chest. "Right here! Where is it?"

I shrugged. There wasn't anything I could do about it now. It was my job to make sure the funeral arrangements were taken care of. Charlotte Rae had taken a vested interest in Ruthie and insisted that she dress Ruthie for the viewing.

A high voice came from behind me. "My-oh-my."

Oh boy.

Standing right in the doorway of the viewing room was all five feet four of Granny.

Zula Fae Raines Payne was the epitome of a true Southern belle. Any insult that came out of

Granny's mouth was often followed up by "bless her heart." Which any Southern woman knew was a phrase used to soften the blow of the previous statement.

Someone could stab Granny in the back and she'd send them a thank-you note.

And I'd put money on it that Granny had already prepared some sort of dish for Ruthie's service tomorrow. That was about the only good thing that happened in a Southern funeral. Whether you were liked or not, all the ladies in the county made sure you went out with a large meal.

"I do love this song." She pranced past me with her head held high. Her short flaming red hair, tousled and mussed up with the perfect amount of gel, complemented her emerald-green dress perfectly.

For a seventy-seven-year-old widow of two, Granny looked great and behaved fifty years younger. The Southern saying "When the husband dies, the widow blossoms like a morning glory" was true with Granny. She looked better than ever and I'd heard she did the same after my grandfather had died. Unfortunately, he passed when I was a baby and I didn't remember anything about him. That was when my parents stepped up and helped Granny run the funeral home.

As she made her way up to the casket, Granny's eyes were on old dead Ruthie. If I didn't know better, I would have sworn Granny had a little bit of a happy twinkle in her eye.

I stepped up beside her. "Granny, what are you doing here?"

Granny didn't say a word, but I remembered exactly what she'd told me after Ruthie had O'Dell Burns wheel Earl out of Eternal Slumber Funeral Home. *Never underestimate a Southern belle.*

The next day she moved her belongings into the Sleepy Hollow Inn and Antiques, right next to Ruthie's room. "We Southern gals don't get mad"—she patted my hand when I tried to stop her from moving out of the funeral home owner's quarters—"we get even."

Ruthie leaned across me, swinging fists in Granny's direction. "You thief! She is a thief! I want her arrested!"

There was no denying what Ruthie's panties were in a wad about. As sure as I was alive, Granny stood over poor old dead Ruthie with a diamond spider brooch neatly pinned on the right side of her dress.

Chapter 3

Have a good night." I waved off the last attendee at Ruthie's visitation and locked the door behind me.

There were a million and one things I needed to do but *that* list was going to have to wait. As much as I didn't want to, I needed to talk to Ruthie and ask her why she believed she was murdered. Ruthie might not have been the most popular citizen in Sleepy Hollow, but she didn't deserve to die . . . or worse, be murdered.

If there was a murderer on the loose—I shuddered thinking about it—he or she needed to be caught. Not that I was a capable of catching anyone, but I certainly could take my concerns to Sheriff Ross.

I slipped back into the viewing room, going from flower arrangement to flower arrangement, pretending to straighten the sympathy cards. People loved to look at the cards to see who they were from.

Believe it or not, someone's status in a small town was often based on the size of the arrangement they sent to the funeral home. Right or wrong, the higher price tag equated to how beloved you were. The larger the floral design, the higher the price tag.

Truth be told, I was procrastinating, working up my nerves to talk to Ruthie.

The funeral home was quiet. Being around dead bodies in caskets really never bothered me. It was a normal daily routine. However, being around a dead body in a casket with its ghost standing next to it was an entirely different story.

"Emma Lee, I'm leaving!" Charlotte hollered through the door from the office, causing me to jump. "I'll see you bright and early."

"Good night!" I yelled loud enough for her to hear me, my voice as shaky as my knees.

I heard Charlotte's high heels click out the door, and the door clicked closed.

Here goes nothing. Where was the Ouija board game when you needed it?

"Ruthie?" The sound of her name as it crossed my lips—and the thought that I was actually trying to talk to her— sent chills up *and* down my spine.

"I'm here." Ruthie stood in the back of the room, nowhere near her casket. "Seeing myself gives me the willies." She shivered. Her jewelry jangled. "Come back here." She waved me over.

"Aren't you supposed to be foggy or see-through?" Wasn't that how ghosts were portrayed in the movies? Sort of free floating?

I straightened some of the chairs on my way to the back of the room, making sure the cream cotton slipcovers were perfectly matched up at the seams. The old wooden folding chairs looked much better covered up, even though they still squeaked when someone sat down.

"That's only in the movies." Ruthie smiled as she squeezed a hair clip back in place. She always wore her hair pinned up on one side.

I smiled back, taking in her hot-pink pajamas and kitty-cat slippers. I just couldn't get used to seeing Ruthie in such an outfit.

"What?" Ruthie looked down at her clothes. She did a little jig. The kitty eyes on her slippers jiggled around.

"I never figured I'd ever see you in kitty slippers." My eyes squinted from the smile that crept up on my face. Ruthie was wealthy. She would never be caught dead in anything other than her fancy jewelry and a cardigan sweater.

"It was late when I got pushed down the stairs. It was bedtime." She brushed her hands down the front of the silk pj's and held her head high. Even in death, Ruthie still had dignity.

"What is this business about you being murdered?" There were no more reasons to beat around the bush.

Her brows snapped downward. "I don't know who did it."

"How do you know someone pushed you?" I remembered the men talking at the funeral. I paused for a moment. "Those steps are steep, and you do have that bad hip."

"Emma Lee Raines, I am not feeble and I did not fall down those steps." She shook her finger at me, and then comically wrapped her hands around her body. She pointed to a spot on the center of her back. "Right here. Right here is where I felt two hands push me."

"And why do you think I can help you?" I dug my finger into my chest. "I'm not a cop. I'm not a private investigator. I'm just a funeral girl."

"Because I know you have access to all the records on the autopsy."

"There wasn't an autopsy."

"What?"

"You fell down the steps. There was no reason for anyone to think anything else."

"I'm telling you, I was murdered." Ruthie's voice escalated. She pointed her bony finger at me. "You are going to help me get to the other side by figuring out who killed me."

"Other side?"

"Great beyond. The light. The big guy in the sky." Ruthie looked up to the ceiling and then back to me. "I can't cross over until I can rest eternal. And that means catching my killer."

"Killer?" The sound of it made me more worried than scared. Was there really a killer on the loose in Sleepy Hollow? Or was there just one person out to get Ruthie Sue Payne, and why?

"Fine." I bit my lip. I couldn't believe what I was about to say. I paused and thought one more second before I spoke. "If trying to find out *who killed you* will get you out of here and not let everyone think I have a case of the 'Funeral Trauma,' I'll do it."

I reached over and picked up one of Ruthie's

memorial cards and the pen from the visitor log. "Tell me what you remember."

"What are you doing?"

"I'm taking notes." I tapped the pen to the card. "This is how I've seen it done on *NCIS*."

Ruthie rolled her eyes. She didn't argue. "I felt something pinch me, like a ring."

"Ring," I stated out loud as I wrote it down. There was no significance to the word, it just seemed like I needed to write it down. "Big hands or small hands?"

I had no idea where I was pulling these questions from, but I needed to gather any information I could. What I really needed to do was go back and watch past episodes of *Ghost Hunter* or *Paranormal Mysteries* to see how they handled ghosts.

"What does that matter? It was two hands." Ruthie shoved her arms out in front of her like she was pushing something. "Wait."

She paced back and forth making the forward pushing motion several times as if she was replaying the incident in her head.

"Hello?" A male voice called out from the vestibule.

I bit my lip. Ruthie was about to tell me something.

Dang. It seemed important too.

"Emma Lee?"

"I'm sorry. The viewing is over for the night," I called out on my way to see who it was. Normally I would let a latecomer visit, but Ruthie was about to tell me something important and this was far from normal.

I stepped out in the foyer to find Sheriff Ross. He was looking official in his Sleepy Hollow brown uniform.

I couldn't help but inwardly swoon when he took off his hat, exposing his high and tight haircut and deep brown eyes. He could rock a five-o'clock shadow like no one's business.

"Hey, Jack." I put my hand on my chest. "You scared me to death. Don't you know how to knock?"

His mouth tilted to the side, giving me an irresistible smirk. In a low Southern drawl he said, "Emma Lee, I saw you through the window talking to someone."

"Me?" I pointed to myself. I shrugged, trying to keep a straight face, "Nope, not talking to anyone."

He put his hat back on and walked past me into the viewing room. He craned his neck as if he was looking for something. He turned around, narrowing his gaze.

Ruthie fluffed her hair. "Whooo-eeeee he sure does come from good stock."

I chuckled and threw my hand to my mouth.

"I . . ." I couldn't tell him about Ruthie's ghost. He would have me committed. It wasn't like we were good friends. He had been popular in school—you know, the hunky athletic type. His crowd didn't hang around the creepy funeral-home girl. "I was singing and cleaning up for the night."

"Were you?" He weaved in and out of the chairs, making his way to the casket. "I didn't know you were a singer."

"I'm not." I ran my hands through my hair. My nerves were shot and standing here with Jack made them even more electric.

"Why did you laugh out loud?"

"Umm . . ." *Great.* He was going to think I was crazy anyway. "I can only imagine how I looked from the outside as I was in here singing my heart out."

He studied me for a moment. I tried to stand still and not give any sort of crazy-girl vibe. Yes, I was going to have to go back and watch some reruns of *NCIS*. They always watched body language, and my insides were like a ball of electricity.

"I went by and saw your granny tonight." He took off his hat again when he stopped at the casket and held it close to his chest. Like a good

Southern gentleman, he was paying his respects to Ruthie. His lips moved like he was saying a silent prayer.

"You did?" I questioned after he turned back around.

Ruthie fanned her hands toward Jack like she wanted me to tell him that she had been murdered. There was no way I was going to do that. Not yet at least, not until I had more information.

"I did. I even had some of that fine sweet iced tea she makes." He grinned. His eyes bored into me. "And some cookies."

Granny could make some dang good tea. She boiled her tea in the same pot, every single time. She claimed it was "seasoned."

"I'm a little curious about her relationship with Ruthie Sue Payne." He rubbed his chin, making a little scratchy noise. "Something isn't right with Ruthie's death. I thought I'd pop over before Zula went to bed to ask a few more questions I had."

"I thought she already told you everything she knew." I ran my hands through my hair. It had been an exhausting day and it only seemed to be getting worse. "Granny came home from the doctor and found Ruthie facedown, nose planted in the worn green carpet at the bottom of the steps."

"It's no secret they weren't close. Enemies in

fact." He pulled out a little notebook. He showed me a page with all sorts of chicken-scratch writing I couldn't make hide nor hair of. "I have a few witnesses that came to me after Ruthie's fall, giving me details of just how much Zula and Ruthie fought."

"Oh, Jack." I brushed past him and pretended to straighten the slipcovers on the back row of chairs. "You can't possibly think that Zula Fae Raines Payne could murder anyone."

"Murder? I didn't say Zula murdered Ruthie." He paused. I could feel him staring at me, and couldn't help but be a little paranoid that he was watching my every move. "I said something wasn't right. Maybe Zula missed something or overheard something. Did Ruthie have a bad hip? Arthritis?"

Ruthie rushed up to him, creating a *whiff* of air.

I shrugged, a little angry at Jack. He might be a cutie patootie, but I suspected he thought my granny was a suspect.

"Do you feel that draft?" Jack put his hands out to see where the puff of air had come from.

"I know he can't see me, but can he feel me?" She tried to blow on him several times. He didn't flinch. "Tell him that I was murdered."

"Draft?" I said through chattering teeth, pretending like I had no clue what he was talking about. I shook my head at Ruthie as she took a seat in the last row. Jack didn't take his eyes off the curtains as he walked over there. He used his hands to feel for a breeze. "What are you, a weathervane?"

"Funny, Emma Lee." He pushed the velvet curtains back and ran his hands along the window. "Strange. It's tight, but you should get that checked out. I bet this old place has some big heating bills."

"Luckily it's spring." My heart fell to my feet when Jack came back and nearly sat right down in Ruthie's lap. I rushed over and grabbed him by the biceps, veering him toward the chairs on the other side of the aisle. "Is this too far back from the viewing? I've been trying to decide if we have too many rows of chairs."

"I really wouldn't have minded that hunk to sit in my lap." Ruthie grinned.

I laughed out loud. I couldn't help it. Jack jerked away.

"Emma Lee, is everything okay?" His dark eyes clouded with suspicion. "You're acting funny."

"I'm fine." I waved off the notion. What I really wanted to say was that I *was not okay*. I could see ghosts.

He didn't look like he believed me. He'd always been pretty smart.

"What were you saying about Granny and this silly notion she had anything to do with Ruthie's death?" I had to change the subject before I cracked and he had me committed.

Ruthie leaned in her chair, taking in our conversation.

"I'm not going to leave any stone unturned." He pulled a piece of paper out of the back pocket of his brown polyester pants and jabbed it toward me. "I'm here to serve you a warrant. I am stopping the funeral."

"For what?" Speechless, I stood there trying to wrap my head around the folded papers he handed me. Warrants were for those types of people who were troublemakers. As far as I knew, I wasn't one.

"Ruthie Sue Payne is not to be buried until I get to examine all the evidence, police reports, autopsy reports and any other reports I deem necessary in order to rule out any foul play." By the look on his face, he was not joking.

"I have to put Ruthie's funeral on hold?" I asked, watching him jot something down on that little pad of paper.

"Yes. That's exactly what I'm telling you." He nodded but continued to write. "Until further notice."

"Further notice?"

"Yep." He tapped the folded paper in my hands with the edge of his pen. "It's all in the warrant."

"That could take days."

"Maybe weeks. Months," he casually said like it was no big deal.

It *was* a big deal. Keeping a body in the refrigerator was not on a funeral-home director's high-priority list.

Ruthie stood up and wrung her hands. Her jewelry jingled. I watched to see if Jack could hear her noisy baubles, but he didn't turn Ruthie's way.

Thinking about keeping Ruthie in the refrigerator made my stomach curl. Especially with no next of kin to claim her.

"I guess you are going to have to figure that one out." He pointed toward the casket. "That is not going anywhere near the ground."

He placed his hat back on his head.

"How do you know it wasn't some random accident or killer on the loose?" I asked. "Think about it. People come in and out of the inn all the time. People we don't know." Granny was always telling me how strange some of the earthy hikers that came to Sleepy Hollow to explore the caves and gorges were.

"I'm checking all of that." He started to walk to

the entrance. "Like I said, no stone unturned. No Ruthie in the ground."

I snarled. He didn't have to talk to me like I was a child and didn't understand what he was telling me. I got it. Ruthie or her ghost was going nowhere until I solved the crime.

"Wait." I jumped in front of him. "What about Granny?"

"I told her to get a lawyer just in case." He reached out and touched my arm. "I adore Zula. But sometimes people do things out of character when they get mad. I'm not saying she did it. But I am saying that something isn't adding up with the whole falling accident." He pointed to his gut. "Call it intuition."

"I told you!" Ruthie stood behind Jack, nodding in agreement over his shoulder. "I was murdered. Ouch." She reached around and pressed on her back. The same place she had told me the hands that shoved her were placed.

"Trust me." He reached out and put his warm, strong hand on my shoulder. Giving it a little squeeze, he said, "I want to prove Zula didn't do it. So make sure she cooperates, and you too."

"We will." I pictured Granny on one side of me and Ruthie on the other. Ruthie's spider brooch began to haunt my memory of Granny wearing it exactly where Ruthie had specifically written in her arrangements. And they really didn't get along.

But murder? No way. Now I had to find out exactly who had done this to Ruthie. Granny's future was at stake. The Sleepy Hollow Inn was the first stop.

Chapter 4

After Jack left, I rushed to my office. Charlotte loved to buy office supplies. She was the only kid I knew who couldn't wait for school to start because she loved getting new paper, pencils and a Trapper Keeper. If I was going to do this detective thing, I could take a lesson or two from Jack. Starting with getting a little notebook out of the supply closet.

I made sure that Jack's cop car was nowhere to be seen when I jumped into the hearse, my ride. It was highly unusual for people to drive a "death coach" around, but I couldn't afford to buy a car, and the hearse got me where I needed to go. And right now I needed to get over to the inn to see Granny.

I looked up and down the street to make sure Jack wasn't parked somewhere, staking out my every move.

It was about as good of a time as any to make a visit to one Zula Fae Raines Payne.

Wincing from stomach pains, I realized I had forgotten to eat, being so busy with the layout and my run-in with Ruthie. I pulled into the local burger joint, getting all sorts of stares from the tourists who had stopped to grab a bite before they headed to the caves.

"What? Haven't you seen a hearse go through a drive-through?" I mumbled and manually rolled down the window as I pulled up to the speaker.

"Can I help you?"

"I'd like a number-two meal with a Coke."

"Pull around."

"That stuff will put you in a pine box like me if you keep it up." Ruthie appeared in the passenger seat.

I jumped. "What are you doing here?"

"I'm going with you to see exactly what kinds of lies Zula Fae is going to tell you."

"She doesn't lie." I pulled up to the window and waited for the fast-food cashier to tell me what I owed. Maybe Granny stretched the truth, but she never lied.

"I want to hear for my own ears what she has to say about me." Ruthie pointed toward the cashier hanging out of the drive-through window with her hand open.

I dropped some money in her palm, waited for my food and finally drove off before I said anything to Ruthie.

"Aren't you supposed to stay at the funeral home?" Wow. The movies really did have this ghost thing all wrong.

"I can go anywhere." She shrugged. "Why would I stay there, when all I care about is figuring out who killed me? The quicker we figure it out, the faster I get to join the love of my life—Earl."

I didn't mention that Earl's love had been my Granny.

"Why do you insist that Granny had anything to do with this?" I reached into the bag and took a handful of fries before turning the hearse on Main Street. With my mouth full, I said, "You are making it very difficult for me to help you if you continue to accuse the people I love."

"I'm not accusing her. All I know is that someone pushed me." She winced, wrapping her hand behind her back. "Zula lives there. She hates me. It's easy to jump to the conclusion that she killed me."

"What's wrong?" I took a sip of Coke and drove around the town square to get to the inn.

"I swear there is some sort of bruise right here." She continued to knead her back. "Can you look and see?"

The thought of looking at what was under Ruthie's pajamas sent chills up my legs. Though it would be interesting to know if she really did have something under there causing her pain. Did ghosts really feel pain? Apparently Ruthie did. Her eyes squinted as she continued to rub.

"It's going to have to wait until later." I gulped down my food before I pulled into the gravel parking lot of the Sleepy Hollow Inn. A flashbulb going off caught my eye and Ruthie's.

The man from Ruthie's visitation, the one who had been sitting with the mayor, was across the street from the inn with a camera in his hand. He jumped back into his Mercedes when our eyes met. He sped off, spitting loose gravel under his tires.

"Do you know that guy?" I asked Ruthie. He definitely wasn't from here. The only person who drove a fancy car like that was Mayor May. She had a fancy PhD from an Ivy League college.

"Never seen him a day in my life." Intensely she stared after the speeding car.

"He was at your visitation." I took one last sip of my Coke and watched the car turn the corner, heading out of town. "He was talking with the mayor about something that is going to be brought up at the council meeting."

"He was probably there because she never has time for anyone and he finally pinned her down at my layout." She tapped her fingernail on the window.

Across the street, I spotted Jack sitting on a bench in the square staring at us . . . me.

I had a feeling he'd show up here.

"I thought he would be watching to see if I came by here." I waved at him. He smiled, melting my heart.

"Do you have a boyfriend?" Ruthie asked.

"No." I turned the car off, grabbed my notepad and opened the door. "Guys think it's a little creepy to date the funeral girl. At least in this small town."

"I'm going to have to take you to a karaoke bar," Jack hollered across the road.

"What?"

"You must love to sing, because you are doing an awful lot of it lately." His smile faded, his eyes hardened. "Are you sure there isn't anything you need to tell me about Ruthie?"

My mouth slammed shut. I was going to have to watch when and where I talked to Ruthie, because Jack was keeping a close eye on me.

Ruthie must've agreed with my dating issues because she didn't say anything. She shuffled her kitty slippers to keep up with me as I headed up the front steps of the inn.

There was nothing like the Sleepy Hollow Inn in the state of Kentucky. The pale yellow brick made the white four-pillar-long veranda stand out. As soon as I stepped on the porch, the tension in my shoulders seemed to fade away, but not Ruthie. She didn't fade anywhere.

Four white rocking chairs on the front porch screamed relaxation and the potted ferns between them were the biggest this side of the state.

Granny said she gave them a sip of tea to help keep them looking so fresh. *Maybe I should be sipping more of Granny's tea and less Coke,* I thought, looking back at Jack.

He gave a slight wave. I turned back around. I didn't mind the attention from him, even if it was under false pretenses.

"Maybe you should do something with your hair." Ruthie reached out. "Don't worry."

"What's wrong with my hair?" I asked under my breath so Jack's supersonic ears couldn't hear me.

"You need an update."

"Update?"

"I think the funeral thing isn't your problem. It's your appearance."

"I thought I heard a car door shut." Granny had pulled open the white double doors and waved me inside the large tan-walled entryway, which smelled of fresh paint. "Come in, come in!"

"You've redecorated!" I said, looking around.

"She didn't waste any time painting over my red walls." Ruthie scowled. She walked around with her mouth open, almost in shock at the changes Granny had already done. "I bet I wasn't even cold when she moved my stuff out."

I wasn't going to tell Ruthie, but the changes did make the place a little more modern.

"What do you think, honey?" Pride shown on Granny's face. "I took out all the old-fogey junk and I'm going to sell it!" She clasped her hands in delight.

"Sell it?" Ruthie screamed, and rushed to Granny's side. "She can't do that! Tell her that she can't sell my things."

Dang! I had completely forgotten to ask Ruthie who her next of kin was. I opened my notebook and jotted down *Ask Ruthie who her next of kin is.*

"Granny?" I shut the front door behind me and

followed her into the front room that was used for a common space for the people staying at the inn. This happened to be my favorite room since it was where Granny kept fresh snacks out throughout the day.

"Yes, honey?" Granny tucked in the edges of the black handkerchief she had tied neatly on her head, which was a sure sign she was in the cooking mood.

I paused when I didn't see the tray of cookies and crackers, and watched Granny sink into a huge stack of cream pillows on a new large brown couch. Her apron flew up in front and she smoothed it down.

"Where is the old furniture?" The new sofa had replaced the old Victorian seating set that had been there for as long as I could remember. "Where're the snacks?"

"Where are my antiques?" Ruthie wrung her hands and walked the floor. Her jewelry clinked.

"Sit still," I whispered, tilting my head to the side so Granny wouldn't hear me.

"I am sitting, honey." Granny's face tightened. "Are you okay?"

"Yes."

"No! You tell her that you are talking to me,

Ruthie Sue Payne." Ruthie pounded her fist in the air. "Ooh, I'd love to get my hands on her!"

"I bet you would." I rolled my eyes.

"What?" Granny stood up, walked over to me and put her hand on my head as if she was checking for a fever. "I think I need to call Doc Clyde."

"No!" I stepped back. "That is the last thing you need to do."

"What is going on with you?" Granny moseyed back over to the couch and flopped down.

Do I tell her or not? I bit the corner of my lip. I walked around the room, taking in all the new items. The red velvet curtains had been replaced by baby-blue floor-to-ceiling drapes, making the windows appear larger. The room definitely looked more inviting.

"Ask her where my things are." Ruthie stood over Granny on the verge of tears. I could only imagine how she felt, coming into a home that she'd owned—well, co-owned—for years and it had all been changed.

"I'm not asking her," I said through gritted teeth.

"That's it." Granny jumped to her feet and rushed out the door into the hallway. "I'm going to get you a cup of tea before I call Doc Clyde."

"Wait!" I called after her. She turned around.

"What did you do with all the antiques? I might be able to use them at the funeral home."

"You don't want that junk." She shooed me off with her hand. "Besides, I buried them deep in that old attic. Don't try to change the subject. I'm still thinking about calling the doc."

Granny didn't wait a minute longer. She headed down the hall quicker than a jackrabbit.

"See what you did?" I pointed to the empty hall. "Now she thinks I've got a case of the 'Funeral Trauma.'"

"Let's go get my antiques."

"If you think I'm going in that creepy old attic, you are crazy." I shook my head. The attic was the scariest place on the earth. There were no lights and no windows. The only way to get to it was through Ruthie's room. In the closet was a door with a skeleton-key lock. No way was I going up there.

I darted down the hallway to the kitchen to try to redeem myself. Granny was fishing around the refrigerator and pulled out a pitcher of tea as I walked in.

"You are either going to have to fix this 'Funeral Trauma' by going to see Doc Clyde and getting a new medicine or learn how to hide your crazy." Granny had a way with words. "I won't be having all of Sleepy Hollow talk about my crazy grand-daughter. We are true Southern women, so start acting like one."

"I'm not crazy," I growled and sat down at the farm table in the middle of the kitchen and sniffed. I was right. Granny was cooking and something good too, making me regret stopping for a burger. "I'm not the Raines the town is going to be talking about."

"What do you mean?" Granny opened the glass door on the corner cabinet where she kept her special tea glasses and grabbed one. She flicked the crushed ice button on the refrigerator door and filled the glass to the rim.

"Sheriff Ross stopped by the funeral home." I watched the ice melt as she poured the tea in the glass. "And it wasn't to visit Ruthie."

Granny placed the glass in front of me and eased down on the bench across from me.

"Did he come for a social call?" She raised her eyebrows up and down in a va-va-voom sort of way.

"No." There was no way Jack was ever going to pay me a social call with the case of crazy that I had. "He was asking all sorts of questions about Ruthie and how she died."

"She fell!" Granny smacked the table.

"Can you remember anything out of the ordinary from that day?" I eased into my line of questioning. "Did she limp? Was she feeling ill?"

"How would I know? I stayed as far away from that woman as I could."

"When you got home from . . ."

"The doctor."

I pulled out the small notepad I had put in my pocket to take notes.

"The doctor, you found her at the bottom of the steps?" *Check to see if Granny was at the doctor's,* I wrote on the notepad.

"Facedown." Granny nodded. "I told Jack . . . er . . . Sheriff Ross, everything I knew."

"She's lying!" Ruthie rushed to my side. "She doing that eye-twitch thing she does when she lies."

"Eye twitch?" I said out loud, and looked at Granny. Sure enough, her left eye was twitching like it had its own heartbeat.

Granny lifted her hand to her eye.

"I do have an eye twitch every once in a while." She spread her eye lid apart like the motion was going to get rid of the twitch.

"Go on." Ruthie coaxed me. "Ask her something you know is a lie."

I took a drink of tea. "Granny, do you remember

my frog you babysat when my parents took me on vacation when I was seven?"

"Yes. Why?" Her eyes narrowed in suspicion. "What does this have to do with crazy old Ruthie?"

Ruthie held her fists up like she was Muhammad Ali. "Let me at her!"

Ignoring Ruthie, I proceeded with my questioning to see if Granny was going to tell me the truth.

"How did it die again?" Not that a frog was the greatest pet in the world. But that was the only pet I was allowed to have. My parents thought owning a cat or dog in the funeral home was not appropriate for the clients. My dad worried the dog would be barking during the services, while Mom worried that cat hair would be all over the caskets. A frog it was.

I clearly remember we got home from vacation, my frog was not in his glass aquarium. Granny told me the frog had died. Years later, out of meanness, Charlotte told me Granny had let the frog go because she couldn't stand it being kept captive.

"I have no idea." Granny folded her hands and put them on the table. Her left eye twitched. "I got up to feed it and it was a goner."

"See! I told you!" Ruthie pointed.

"Why are you asking about that silly frog?" Granny asked. Her eyes widened as she looked over my shoulder toward the oven. "My casserole!" She got up and brushed her hands down her apron before she walked over to the oven.

Smoke poured out when she opened the door. I could never recall a time Granny had burned anything. *Burned casserole for first time*, I wrote in the notepad to remind myself to mentally go back through our conversation and see exactly where Granny had gone mushy-brained and forgotten about the casserole.

"Child, you caused me to forget all about my chicken-and-green-bean casserole." She waved the oven mitt in front of her face to clear the smoke. Not only was the food as black as night, so was the dish.

Granny didn't bother with trying to save any of it. She dumped the entire thing in the sink.

"Who was that for?" I asked. Granny only made that particular dish for certain occasions.

"I had planned on taking it to Ruthie's funeral tomorrow."

Yep, all good Southern women, whether they liked you or not, brought food to a funeral.

"She knows I can't stand chicken-and-green-bean casserole." Ruthie pinched her nose as if with a clothespin. "She always wanted to make it for the people staying at the inn, but I never let her. *Harrumph.*"

"Which reminds me." Granny's burnt food brought me back to the real reason I was here. "Jack seems to believe you know more about Ruthie's death than you are letting on."

"He didn't say that to me." She hurried around her kitchen. There was definitely something going on in her head, because she was doing a good job of ignoring me.

"He told me that he told you to get a lawyer."

"He did? Hmm. I don't recall." Granny looked up to the ceiling as if she were really thinking about it. But I knew better. Granny really should have been an actress.

"Granny?" I needed her to look at me.

"What?" She stopped and turned. Her eye was twitching again.

"Lie!" Ruthie screamed and pointed.

"He served me a warrant." I rubbed my head. It was beginning to hurt. Trying to keep up with two conversations at the same time was exhausting.

"He arrested you?" She gasped.

"No." I shook my head. "The warrant was to stop Ruthie's funeral until he investigates her suspicious death a little further."

"She fell!" Granny untied the apron and threw it on the table. No eye twitch this time.

Changing the subject at this point was a good idea. Granny was getting irritated not only by my line of questioning, but by the fact that her casserole was burnt. She didn't seem to be worried about Ruthie's funeral being stopped. She didn't question me any further. Nor did she seem to care that Jack thought she might be a suspect.

Regardless, another ten minutes of idle chitchat and I said good-bye. There was a little sneaky suspicion in my gut that Granny would be making me a visit with some more information that she wasn't quite willing to give up . . . yet, anyway.

"I'm telling you she is hiding something." Ruthie tapped her kitty slipper on the passenger-side floorboard. "I could always tell when Zula Fae was lying by that darned ol' eye twitch of hers."

I glanced in my rearview mirror to make sure no one, including Jack, was watching me before I spoke.

"I can't get over it." I shook my head, keeping my eyes on the road. "I have never noticed that little quirk about Granny before."

There was no denying it. Granny was hiding something, but what?

"I have no doubt that she found you facedown

at the bottom of the steps and believes that you fell." I recalled Granny's eyes when I asked her about Ruthie and there was no eye twitch. I pulled the hearse in the garage behind the funeral home.

Both of us walked in silence going into the funeral home. Ruthie looked like she was still contemplating what I had said about Granny believing Ruthie fell. If Ruthie's theory about Granny's eye twitch was true, Granny was telling the truth. Whether Ruthie liked it or not, Zula Fae Raines Payne did not push her down the steps.

Chapter 5

Last night my mind wouldn't slow down long enough for me to get any sort of sleep. With Ruthie's little bombshell of being murdered, Jack stopping the funeral, and Granny as a potential suspect, my mind was reeling with how I was going to solve all of these problems.

During the midnight hours, I went over my notes several times. I had nothing written down that was going to give me any clues about who murdered her. All I had was a bunch of questions with no answers.

There was one person who did have the answers. Ruthie.

Who was her next of kin? Did she have any fights with anyone recently? Did she know of anyone who wanted to get rid of her . . . permanently?

Dom, dom, dom. Chopin's "Funeral March" chimed on my cell. I didn't recognize the number and quietly prayed it wasn't about another dead body. The thought of a real serial killer didn't make me feel better. Besides, I didn't have time to do another funeral. My time needed to be spent getting Granny off the hook and Ruthie to the other side.

"Hello?" I answered.

"Is it true that Ruthie Sue Payne's funeral has been put on hold?" Mayor May frantically questioned me. I was positive she wasn't winking and waving on the other end of the phone.

Funeral! I smacked my head and looked up at the clock on my office wall. It was ten minutes till show time and last night I had completely forgotten to put in a late-night call to the *Sleepy Hollow Journal* so they would publish the cancellation of Ruthie's funeral in the paper for all the citizens to see. I set my notebook on my desk and got up.

"Yes, Mayor May," I confirmed and peeked around the door into Charlotte's office, where she was talking to a grieving family about some arrangements. Charlotte glanced up, and I motioned for her to come here and mouthed *now*.

I grabbed the warrant off my desk and clutched the papers.

"Was anyone going to say something?" Mayor May was not happy. "I am a busy woman. And I would have wasted not only my time, but the taxpayers' money, if I had not run into Sheriff Ross."

If she already knew, then why did she call me? To let me know that I screwed up again? Regardless, I'm glad she did. It prevented an even bigger mess.

"I'm sorry, Mayor." All I could do was apologize. The wrath of Charlotte might put me right next to Ruthie if I didn't come up with a solution . . . and fast!

The mayor ranted and raved a few more seconds about how this would have never happened if my parents and Granny were still running the funeral home. She threatened to call my parents, as if they were going to ground me or something, before she slammed down her phone.

Now I was beginning to realize why my parents took early retirement and moved to Florida, leaving Charlotte and me to run the place.

I rushed into Charlotte's office without knocking, without thinking.

"Oh." I stopped and looked at the two gentlemen in there. They were dressed in black suits and each of them had a black briefcase on his lap. Each looking more official than the other. And both serious.

"Yes, Emma Lee?" Charlotte acted like I had ruined her life by just breathing.

"Can I please see you out here?" I pointed behind me into the hallway.

"Excuse me." Charlotte apologized to the gentlemen like I probably should have. She stood up and planted a smile on her face. She rubbed her hands together. "I'll be right back."

"This better be good, for you to call me out of a potential client," Charlotte whispered in my ear. She wasn't happy either.

"Who are they?" I asked.

"Emma Lee, I'm in the middle of my job. Is there something that you need?"

"You are going to *kill me*." I glanced over Charlotte's shoulder. Ruthie was standing behind her. I handed Charlotte the wadded-up paper with the Sleepy Hollow Sheriff's logo.

We were familiar with the sheriff's logo because some families wanted records of a loved one's autopsy and it required a warrant.

"Oh my God, Emma." Her brow creased with worry. "The next thing out of your mouth, I pray, is that you called the *Journal* last night after this happened."

Slowly I shook my head.

"Ahh, oh," Ruthie said, and backed away from Charlotte. Nervously, she picked at the edges of her gray hair, which hung loosely, perfectly framing her petite face. Her bracelets jingled around her small wrists.

For a split second, I thought Charlotte's head was going to spin around and fly right off her shoulders.

But it didn't.

"You have no idea how important it is for us to *not* make any mistakes." She closed her eyes. She spoke in an odd, yet gentle tone, "I'm going to go to the bathroom to compose myself. When I come out, you better have a typed note on the door and be ready to answer any questions from the good citizens of this fine community."

She turned on her heels, her long, red, luscious curls flung in the air, landing perfectly on her back as she made her way to the restroom.

"You better watch out for her," Ruthie warned and gazed at Charlotte with a bland half smile. "She's the spitting image of your grandfather, with the wit and charm of Zula."

Ruthie was right. Zula and Charlotte had Southern charm with a venomous tongue. Everything was great, if everything went their way. You better watch out if things didn't. Business dealings were no different.

Charlotte didn't care about poor Ruthie's body in a freezer for God knew how long. All she cared about was the fact the town was going to see this as a big mistake on the funeral home's part, which the mayor had already confirmed. Now it was my job to figure out how to fix it.

I headed back to my office. There were only a few more minutes until the Eternal Slumber Funeral Home was supposed to be hosting the goodbye ceremony for Ruthie Sue Payne, which meant that there was no time to print a letter like Charlotte wanted me to. I grabbed the tape dispenser off my desk and rushed out to the front door.

"There." I smoothed out the wrinkles and put tape on each corner of the warrant, taping it to the door. I brushed my hands together and made sure the door was locked.

I stood in the vestibule long enough to see a few people show up and try to open the door along with a few curse words. I was sure I heard my name and "Funeral Trauma" thrown in under their breath after they read the posted paper.

"It won't be long now," I whispered and pulled the front room's curtain back just enough to watch an angry five-foot-six Beulah Paige Bellefry shake a fist at the funeral home before she stomped back to her red Cadillac.

At the ripe old age of forty-two years, Beulah was the youngest woman in the Auxiliary group. She was also the fashionista of Sleepy Hollow, with her fake lashes and tan.

Beulah Paige was second only to Ruthie in the gossip department. Since Ruthie was dead, it was Beulah Paige's time to shine.

She would have the news of the warrant spread all over town, like wildfire, before I would even make it back to my desk.

I'd put a bet on it that she was planning on being the first Auxiliary member at the funeral so she could get a front-row seat and watch everyone come in, and then go back and share everything she saw with the ladies in the Auxiliary. She'd supply them with plenty of gossip for the next month or until something better came along.

"Nice move." Ruthie appeared next to me and pointed toward Beulah, zooming off in her red Caddy. "With Beulah in charge, now everyone in Sleepy Hollow is going to know I was murdered.

You know, she's been dying to take my spot in the Auxiliary."

"I never thought of that. I simply wanted everyone to know that your funeral has been put on hold."

"My funeral on hold?" She pointed at the viewing room. "You mean on ice?"

John Howard Lloyd and Vernon Baxter had moved Ruthie's casket back onto a church truck and was wheeling her down the center aisle to take her back down to the refrigerator in the basement.

"Mornin', Ms. Emma." John Howard grinned a big, gummy openmouthed smile and patted down the top of his hair. No matter how much he patted that wiry mess, it wasn't going to cooperate. "Ms. Charlotte told me to move poor ol' Ruthie's body to the refrigerator."

I'll never forget the first time I met John Howard. He looked like he had one foot in the grave. He came to the funeral home without a tooth in his head and that crazy hair sticking up all over, but he needed a job. Granny immediately put him to work digging graves and doing odd jobs around the funeral home.

"Yes, thank you." I smiled, giving him the go-ahead to take the body. "Can you please put a blanket on top before you close the refrigerator door?"

He looked like he was weighing what I had said before he pushed the cart down the hall.

Ruthie stood next to me in silence, never once taking her eyes off the casket being rolled away. The only sound was the creak of the steel wheels trying to make it over the thick-threaded carpet with each turn.

John Howard stopped and only turned his neck to look at me.

"Do you think there is a killer out there?"

"I'm not sure, John Howard." I shook my head and tried to ease his fears. "I guess I really shouldn't have posted the warrant."

He continued to push the casket and finish the task Charlotte had bestowed on him.

I walked back over to the door and peeled the warrant off of it. The chattering crowd down the street caught my eye.

Several people were gathered in front of Artie's Meats and Deli next to Beulah's big red Cadillac. Beulah stood in the middle, mouth flapping, waving her hands in the air, telling the grandest tale.

"Hmm . . ." Ruthie's eyes narrowed, taking in the scene.

I could see it now. Everyone running to Artie's to stock up on ammunition or get a new gun because I had put fear in them by taping the warrant to the door. "Posting this was probably not the best idea."

"Probably not." Sheriff Jack Henry Ross leaned against the wall with his arms crossed. He peered at me, intently.

My heart jolted as my pulse pounded.

"Jack Henry!" I jumped around, running my hands through my hair. What if Ruthie was right and my stuck-in-the–nineties hairdo was the problem of all of my dating issues? "What are you doing here?"

I walked past him and down the hall toward my office. He wasn't far behind.

"The phone at the station has been ringing off the hook. So I decided to come down here and see what all the commotion was about." His jaw clenched. He leaned up against the office door. He was not amused. "Now my officers have to spend time reassuring everyone that there is not a serial killer running the streets of Sleepy Hollow."

As much as I wanted to hear what he was saying, I hated myself for focusing on his lips and remembered the most embarrassing moment I had ever had.

Look away. My mind told me to stop staring, but my eyes wouldn't listen. *Remember the past.* I repeated in my head and walked behind the desk and sat in my chair.

No matter how much I tried to forget the time Jack Henry and I almost kissed in high school during an intense game of spin the bottle and how awful the situation was, I could barely resist the urge to kiss him now.

"Mayor May gave me an earful at Higher Grounds Café." He held up a paper cup. "When I told her the funeral was not going to happen today."

"After I got home from visiting Granny, I completely forgot to call the *Journal*." I forced my eyes to look at my empty coffee mug sitting on my desk. I had to get out of there and get myself together. Why did Jack Henry have to be one of those guys who got better-looking with age? Grabbing my mug, I got up. "Do you want a refill?"

"Sure." He handed me his cup. His fingers brushed up against mine. Electricity spread across all my nerve endings.

"I will be right back." I could feel my cheeks ball up and I tried not to smile, but lost all control. I couldn't get out of there fast enough.

"You've got it bad." Ruthie rushed to my side

and walked behind me all the way to the kitchen.

The funeral-home kitchen was basic, with a refrigerator, stove and microwave, and we had to
clean our own dishes in the single sink that sat
under the only window in the room. We used an
old cupboard we bought at the Goodwill for storage after we cleaned it up.

The kitchen really wasn't bad. Charlotte found
a cute wooden café table with four bar chairs and
sat it in the middle of the room for us to eat on.

If we were working on a body, we were all
here, so we would try to eat family style. My little
funeral-home family.

"I don't have anything bad." I denied my attraction to Jack Henry. I was never good at covering
up my feelings. I clamped my mouth shut when
Mary Anna Hardy, the funeral-home hair stylist
and makeup artist, walked into the kitchen.

"You don't have what bad?" Mary Anna put
a wonky eye on me when she saw me talking to
myself. She looked around. Her empty mug dangled from a finger. "Who are you talking to?"

Mary Anna Hardy owned Girl's Best Friend
Spa, the only hair salon in Sleepy Hollow. Even
though she had a staff of eight hairdressers, she
was the only one weird enough to do hair on dead
people.

"I heard you coming, and I do have something bad." I grabbed a handful of my limp brown hair and flipped it in the air. "I have bad hair and wanted to see if you could do something with it."

"Really?" Mary Anna's blue eyes opened with shock. She rushed over in her hot-pink high heels and stuck her hands in my hair. I couldn't help but look down at her big boobs toppling out of her white V-neck. Her short bleached blond hair was styled exactly like Mary Anna's icon, Marilyn Monroe. Mary Anna was never seen without a pair of high heels. It didn't matter if she was going to Artie's to grab toilet paper and had on sweat pants. She lived by the dead icon's words *Give a girl the right pair of shoes and she will conquer the world.*

"I've been dying to get my hands on these boring strands." She put her hands together and raised them to the sky as if God had just answered her prayers.

"Boring?"

Ruthie stood next to Mary Anna with a huge smile on her face. "Told you."

"You would look great with some fresh highlights and a little layering." She continued to fluff my hair. "Yes, layers. Maybe some big bangs."

"I think she's right." Ruthie nodded. "Highlights are exactly what you need to make a change."

"No bangs. Nothing big," I protested, instantly regretting the lie I told Mary Anna. I didn't want her to touch my hair now or ever. Who cared if I was boring? Certainly not the dead people I worked with.

"I will put you down for noon tomorrow at the salon." She bounced on her toes, she was barely able to contain her excitement. She grabbed the coffeepot and filled her mug to the brim, and took a few sips out of it to make room for the five spoons of sugar she dumped in. "Gotta stay awake to keep up with the dead." She winked before she walked out.

"I'm so glad you are going to get your hair done," Ruthie said.

I glanced around the kitchen and down the hall to make sure we were alone.

"This is not what you think it is." I flipped up the edge of my hair. "I had to think quick on my feet when she came in. People are going to think I'm crazy if they keep seeing me talking to you . . . talking to the air."

I filled up my mug and Jack Henry's cup.

"Fine." Ruthie shrugged. "You won't regret it. Especially after the cute sheriff sees it."

I ignored her and walked back to my office, stopping briefly on the outside of my door to watch Charlotte and the two businessmen at the front door.

"Be sure to give me a call," one of the men said and handed Charlotte what looked like a business card.

"We would like to resolve this matter quickly and quietly," Charlotte assured them as she shook their hands.

I ducked into my office before she saw me spying on her.

The last thing I needed was for her to come into my office to give me "the business" about forgetting to call the *Journal* to cancel Ruthie's funeral.

"Here you go." I walked over to the chairs in front of my desk where Jack Henry was sitting.

"Who is Ruthie's next of kin?" His eyebrows lifted and then he took a sip.

"I have no idea." I shook my head. I tried to straighten my cluttered desk so I could set my mug down. "There isn't any record that I could find."

"Didn't you ask her?" He set his cup down, leaned back in the chair before he crossed his arms and stared at me.

The muscles in my hand gave out and the mug

went crashing down on my desk, coffee spilling all over the place.

"Oh!" I grabbed a handful of Kleenex sitting on the credenza behind my desk and tried to soak up the coffee that landed all over my paperwork and files.

Did I ask her? His words rang in my head. What did he mean, did I ask her?

My eyes scanned my messy desk for my detective notebook as I piled files on top of each other. It had to be here somewhere.

"Are you looking for this?" Jack Henry's eyes danced around my face in amusement. He held my little spiral pad in his fingertips.

Chapter 6

How could I be so stupid? I questioned myself. I knew better than to leave it sitting out for all the world to see.

"That's mine!" I leaned over the desk, files tumbling to the floor, and grabbed it from him.

"Doing a little detective work?" A shadow of annoyance crossed his face. He stood up and picked up the messy file off the floor.

"I'm . . ." I thumbed through the notebook, looking for anything that might have tipped him off to Ruthie's ghost.

"You see Ruthie, don't you?" With his hand planted firmly on the desk, he leaned over and whispered, "You don't have 'Funeral Trauma,' do you?" His air quotes sort of annoyed me.

I sank into my desk chair and clutched my notebook. Ruthie stood next to Jack with her eyes wide open, begging me to tell him. She looked like she was holding her breath, waiting for me to spill it.

"I . . ." I hesitated.

"There are things in that little notebook of yours that only Ruthie would know, and she's dead." He rolled his eyes and plunged his hands in his uniform pants pockets.

"Tell him!" Ruthie's hand flew up in the air and she stomped around. "You can help him and get closer to him at the same time," she chirped.

"Yes. I see Ruthie," I blurted. I could see on his face that he thought I was two cups of crazy. Scratch that. Make it a full pot of crazy. There was no hiding the crazy now. "She . . . she's standing next to you in hot-pink pajamas and kitty cat slippers." I pointed to the left of him.

He jumped right, facing what to his left. "Th . . . th . . . there?" He stuttered and pointed to the empty space in front of him.

He reached down, grabbed the chair and held it like a shield between him and Ruthie.

"Yes."

"Pink pajamas and kitty slippers?"

"Hot pink." I took the chair from his grip and put it back where it belonged.

Ruthie bounced around in joy.

"But that's not what she was wearing when she died." He ripped the Velcro pocket open on his uniform jacket and pulled out his notebook. "Right here, she was wearing a black button-up cardigan, flat black shoes, pink capri pants and a sleeveless blouse under the cardigan."

Ruthie listened to the list of items she had been wearing when they found her. "No, that is not right." Ruthie refuted what he was saying. "I was in bed and heard a noise. I went to the top of the steps and hollered for Zula. That's when someone pushed me."

"What? Is she talking to you?" Jack questioned me. I was turned in Ruthie's direction and paid him no attention.

It was difficult to have two conversations. One with the living. One with the dead.

"Emma Lee?" Jack Henry was trying to get my attention. I was sure I looked crazy, looking at thin air, when I was actually watching Ruthie.

"She said that she was in her pj's when she heard a noise. She went to the top of the stairs and that was when someone pushed her." I conveniently left out the Zula part, because Ruthie and I had already established that Granny was telling the truth by her eye-twitch method. Plus, I didn't want to give Jack any more information that could hurt Granny.

"Are you telling me that someone took the time to change her out of her pajamas after they killed her, and then put her in regular clothes?" Jack eyed me and then looked at the space next to him as if he was giving Ruthie the same look.

Ruthie nodded.

"Yes."

"But why would they do that?" He asked a very good question.

"I don't know." I paced in front of the desk between Jack and Ruthie. Glancing at her, and then at him. "You are the sheriff, not me."

I snapped my fingers.

"Why would someone take the time to change her clothes?" I grabbed a pen and my notebook. I wrote down what Ruthie had said, word for word, except the part about Granny.

"Ask her." Jack nodded.

"Ask her what?"

"Ask her if someone switched out her clothes."

I looked at Ruthie. I didn't have to ask her. "She can hear you."

"I don't know," she said. "When I died, I followed the signs that told me how to get on the other side. Once there they told me to go back. By the time I got back, I was here." Ruthie stomped a kitty slipper on the ground.

"She said that she went somewhere in the universe," I waved my hand in the air, "and they sent her back. When she got back, she was here."

He threw back his head and let out a great peal of laughter.

"What?" I shook my head. "You think I'm crazy and this was all a big joke to you. Well, I'm not crazy Jack Henry, *Sheriff* Ross. So go on. Call Doc Clyde and tell him I'm all primed for the nut house!"

"Stop." He was bent over, holding his stomach. His laughter was a full-hearted sound. "The crazy thing is, I believe you."

I tried to suppress a giggle once Ruthie clasped her hands together in delight and gave a little chuckle.

"What's going on in here?" Charlotte stood in the doorway, unamused. "Oh, *you're* here."

"Good to see you too, Charlotte." Jack took his hat off and greeted her like a good Southern boy and then put it back on.

"Are you here to stop another funeral, Sheriff Ross?" Sarcasm dripped off her lips. She folded her arms across her body.

The quick moment he took his hat off, I noticed

he put in a little more hair gel, making him look very GQ. I liked it.

"Nope. Just here to ask Emma Lee if she wants to go to the karaoke bar tonight." He gave an irresistibly devastating grin.

My eyes widened.

Charlotte lifted her perfectly waxed eyebrow into a shocked surprise. She turned on her heels and clicked back down the hallway to her office.

"Did you see her face?" I laughed. Charlotte and I both knew that Jack was not there to ask me out, but it was worth seeing the look on her face.

"What?" Jack shrugged. "I'm not kidding. Since you sing and all."

"I don't. I was talking to Ruthie all of those times." There was no way, no how I was going to go to a karaoke bar and make a bigger fool of myself. "I am not going to any karaoke bar."

"Oh, yes you are, Emma Lee Raines," Ruthie protested. "You are going to get your hair fixed and go to that bar."

"What? Did Ruthie say something?" Jack asked.

"No." I shook my head. Ruthie was right. It was high time this funeral girl got a taste of life. "Not tonight. Tomorrow, pick me up at eight."

"Why not tonight?"

"Because I have a murder to solve."

He smirked. "Emma Lee, you leave the detective work up to the police. I'll let you know the questions I need to ask Ruthie and you give me the answers. Got it?"

"Got it," I lied.

There was no turning back now. I had to figure out how to get Ruthie to the other side and Granny off the hook.

"Tomorrow night at eight," he confirmed. "I'm going back to the inn to see if they found any prints."

"Prints?"

"After I saw you at the inn, I figured you went there to snoop, so I put a warrant on Ruthie's room to check for prints."

"I'm telling you Granny didn't do it." No matter how cute he was and how much my heart fluttered when he looked at me, I wasn't going to stand for him accusing Granny.

"I never said she did. But those pajamas have to be somewhere." He darted out the door.

Hmm . . . I had never thought of that. Where were Ruthie's hot-pink pajamas and kitty slippers?

I wrote the new discoveries in my notebook. If I find the pj's, I find the killer.

One thing Granny said that didn't add up and haunted me was that she had just gotten home from the doctor's. Ruthie said that she was in bed. Why was Granny at the doctor's at night?

As far as I knew, Doc Clyde only kept daytime office hours.

Go see Doc Clyde, I wrote in my notebook. *See if Granny did go to the doctor and why she went to see the doctor.*

"By the way . . ." I turned back to ask Ruthie if she knew something that someone wouldn't want her to know that would give them a reason to kill her, but she was gone.

Quickly I wrote my question in the notebook, before putting it in my purse. I grabbed my phone.

"Time to go play crazy," I whispered, and then stopped by Charlotte's office.

I rapped on her office door. She was hunched over a file on her desk and clicked away on a calculator.

"What?" She snarled, and didn't bother to look up.

"I'm going to see Doc Clyde."

"Good! You need to," she snapped.

Chapter 7

Emma Lee, what are you doing here?" Ina Claire Nell slid open the receptionist glass, and then looked up at the clock. It was already past noon and I still hadn't figured out anything new on who killed Ruthie or why.

"I wanted to talk to the doc." I rolled up and down on my toes. After I got to see Granny's file, I'd spend the rest of the day working on the few leads I had written down about Ruthie's murder. But figuring out why Granny was with Doc Clyde in the middle of the night seemed a lot easier than finding a killer.

Ina Claire's hands were a little shaky as she thumbed through the schedule book on the counter searching the names of appointments. Nervously, she fiddled with fallen strands of hair from her blond frosted updo and whispered, "Do you have an appointment?"

I looked around the waiting room, which consisted of two wooden chairs with padded cushions tied to them and a stack of old *Southern Living* magazines on the table between them. Maybe Granny needed to come over here and do a little redecorating. The plain beige walls screamed of needing some color.

The only other person in there was Hettie Bell, the streetwise girl who Ruthie and Granny had given a job to a few months ago at the inn. Telling by Hettie's black pants, black sweater and thick black eyeliner, she needed Doc Clyde way more that I needed him. At least I didn't dress crazy.

We made eye contact for a brief moment before she looked down, her long, straight black hair cascading in front of her eyes. She played with her fingers.

Hhmph. Ina Claire got my attention by clearing her throat.

"No," I whispered. With a sense of urgency and a little hint of crazy, my eyebrows lifted upward. "I *need* to see him, if you know what I mean."

"Oh." Slowly Ina Claire nodded and pushed her glasses farther up on her nose and tucked the stray hairs back into a bobby pin. "Ho . . . hold on." She slid the glass window closed like she could breathe in my crazy "Funeral Trauma" germs. Ina Claire couldn't get out of her swiveling chair fast enough.

In the meantime, I sat down next to Hettie.

"Hi," I said. She didn't look up—only scooted her chair away from me. "Don't you work at the inn with my granny?"

"What's it to you?" She glanced over at me.

"I was just making some idle chitchat." I grabbed one of the magazines that was dated five years ago and flipped through it. "What do you do at the inn anyway?"

"I'm not interested in *idle chitchat*."

"Okay." I planted my elbow on the chair arm closest to Hettie and leaned way over. "Then let's get down to the nitty gritty. Is there anything strange going on at the inn? Was there anyone unusual there the week Ruthie died? Anyone that looked suspicious?"

Hettie didn't move. It was like she was digesting all the questions I had just thrown at her.

She used her hands and parted her hair, throwing it over her shoulders. She glanced at the receptionist window, and then to me.

"I did see this man, in a suit, come around a

few times over the last couple of months to see Zula. She made sure Ruthie was gone every single time." Hettie started to talk very fast when we heard Ina Claire's footsteps were coming closer. "I don't think Ruthie knew about this guy because Zula asked me to keep tight lipped." Hettie shrugged. "So I did. Then there was this time a couple weeks ago where this interior decorator stopped by because Zula asked her to come by. All the way from Lexington too."

Interesting.

"One problem." Hettie's eyebrows rose in amusement. "Zula wasn't there when the decorator came. Only Ruthie. And you should've seen Ruthie's face when that woman said who she was."

I could only imagine. I laughed.

"Needless to say, that woman didn't wait around." Hettie straightened up and went back to ignoring me when we heard Ina Claire's footsteps coming back down the hall toward the waiting room.

Ina Claire didn't bother looking at Hettie. She glared at me.

"Hi." I wiggled my fingers in the air, and then pointed to the empty chair next to me as if something or someone was next to me. "Can you get her an appointment too?"

"Who, Emma Lee?" Doc Clyde appeared in the doorway that led to the single exam room.

"Me!" I jumped up and pushed my way past him, leaving Hettie and Ina Claire with their mouths gaped open. There was silence until I reached the exam room and hopped up on the paper-lined table, and then I heard them down the hall.

"I will not be in the same room with someone who thinks she can see dead people." Hettie Bell's whisper was not a whisper anymore. "That girl is crazy!"

"Now, now, Hettie," I could hear Doc Clyde trying to soothe her. There were a few mumbles that I couldn't understand.

Why was Hettie there? Who was Hettie really? I grabbed my notebook out of my purse and jotted down these questions. Hettie Bell showed up out of the blue one day and the next thing I knew, she was working at the inn.

I had never questioned Granny about her. Like Granny would say, it was Hettie's tale to tell and I should just sit on mine, which meant that it was none of my business. Hettie was a little scary with all her black, but it wasn't unusual for those types to come to the area to explore caves and do whatever they do around campfires.

I quickly put my notepad back in my purse and used the pen to make stick figures on the white paper I was sitting on.

Doc Clyde told Ina Claire to take Hettie next door for a soda at Higher Grounds, and then I heard Doc Clyde's old brown doctor shoes dragging on the grungy carpet.

Surely Doc Clyde would think I was there for the "Funeral Trauma" and not there to try and read Granny's records.

"Emma Lee, so glad to see you." Kindly, his eyes had a deep set of worry in them. He shut the door behind him. "What brings you here without an appointment today?"

He glanced at the stick figures, brushed his thinning hair to the side and then looked back at me.

"I wanted to talk to you about my medicine." I punched my finger in the paper and created a big hole, pretending to be a little crazy. It wasn't like I was taking those little pills he had given me for the "Funeral Trauma," but it was a good excuse to try to get a look into Granny's file.

"All right. I need to get your file." He opened the door.

"Wait!" I stopped him. I needed him to be out of the office in order for me to get a look into

Granny's records. "I want one of them sodas you sent Hettie and Ina Claire to get. I feel like I might pass out." I knew he didn't keep soda in the office.

Doc Clyde held his pointy chin up in the air and let out an awkward cough. "How about water?"

"No!" I started twitching. "I need caffeine."

He drew in a deep breath. "Fine. I'll be right back." He left the room.

"Thanks!" I screamed and waited for the front office door to click shut before I jumped off the exam table.

The files were kept in a pantry type closet behind Ina Claire's desk. It wasn't brain science to look for Granny's file. It was alphabetized.

"What are you doing?" Ruthie came up behind me, peering over my shoulder.

"Ruthie!" I nearly jumped out of my skin. "You have got to start announcing yourself and stop scaring me."

"And how am I supposed to do that?" Ruthie asked, tapping her kitty slippers on the old tile floor.

"I don't know. Maybe ring a bell or something." I thought it sounded like a good suggestion. "I know! How about a bell like a cat wears to warn the birds?"

"Emma Lee, I can't get a bell. I'm dead, in case

you have forgotten," she chided, each word heavily laced with sarcasm. "Now, what are you doing? You can't go reading private files. The last thing I need is for you to be put in the slammer."

"I don't intend to go to the slammer." I shut the drawer and gripped Granny's file. "I got what I needed."

She scanned the file's label.

"And just how is Zula's file going to help solve my murder?"

"She claims she was at the doctor's office and when she got back to the inn, you were dead." I shook the file in the air. "Doc Clyde keeps meticulous records and if she was here, then it would be in this."

"You put that back." Ruthie scolded me like she was my own Granny. "This is a federal offense."

"Says who?" *Was I really arguing with a ghost?*

I knew figuring out who killed Ruthie was my number-one priority, but Granny's health was just as important.

"Besides, it will only take a second to see why Granny was here." I threw my hands up in the air. "I promise to devote the rest of my free time figuring out who the murderer is."

"If they find out you took the file . . ." She shook

her finger at me. "Besides, we already know that Zula didn't kill me."

Was Granny sick? I had to find out the answer. "Me taking a tiny peek at her file will let me know why she was here."

"If Zula wanted you to know why she went to see Doc Clyde, she would've told you." Ruthie came closer and grabbed the edge and pulled. "Now, put it back!"

"No!" I pulled harder, forcing her to release the file.

Ignoring her, I raced back to the exam room after I heard faint whispers coming from outside of the doctor's office front door. I put Granny's file deep in my purse and made sure I planted my butt in the crease of the white paper so Doc Clyde didn't think I got up.

"Here you go, Emma Lee." Doc Clyde held out a Coke can when he came back into the room.

"No." I shook my head. "I don't drink that. I wanted diet."

He extended his arm fully and held it out farther. "This is what I bought and it's all I've got."

"No thanks. I'll go get what I want." I jumped off the table in protest and grabbed my purse.

"Where are you going, Emma Lee?" Doc Clyde

stood firm in front of the door with his arms crossed.

"I'm feeling much better." I smiled, throwing my purse over my shoulder. "I think it's seasonal allergies." I scratched my nose and desperately tried to ignore Ruthie.

"It's a case of liar-liar pants on fire." Ruthie stood in the corner of the exam room where the ear thingies hung on the wall next to the blood pressure cuff.

"Ina Claire said that you had someone else with you," Doc Clyde said.

"There is. Me!" Ruthie jumped up and down waving her arms. There was definitely nothing wrong with her physical abilities.

"Ina Claire needs her head checked out worse than me." I looked around. "Do you see someone? I don't."

"A . . . no, but . . ." Doc Clyde paused.

"But nothing." I pushed past him. Ina Claire jumped back from the wall in the hallway where she was clearly listening to our conversation. I pointed at her. "Your turn."

Ina Claire glared at me with reproachful eyes. "I don't know what you are up to, Emma Lee, but you sure can bet that I'm going to be putting a call in to Zula Fae and Charlotte Rae."

"You know their numbers!" I made it to the waiting room where Hettie was sitting, still slumped over with her hair down in her eyes. I could feel Ina Claire coming up behind me. Ruthie sat in the chair next to Hettie. I pointed to it. "There you are."

"There's who, Emma Lee?" Ina Claire asked. She wrung her hands. "Emma, are you having a hallucination?"

"Come on let's go." I motioned for Ruthie, and then looked at Hettie. "Girl, you better run out of here or they will have you committed looking like that."

"Doc! Doc!" Ina Claire rushed in her office and slid the receptionist glass door closed. Only she slammed it, shattering it into tiny pieces all over the floor, before she ran to the back to find Doc Clyde. "Emma Lee is acting crazy!"

"Oh, shiny like stars!" I hollered. If I was going to play crazy, I'd better do a good job.

"See ya," I patted my purse and waved over my shoulder before heading out the door. I had a town council meeting to get to.

Chapter 8

A mazing grace how sweet the sound, chimed out of my phone, reminding me that the city council meeting was tonight.

Funeral hymns were the only ringtones I had on my phone. It was a company phone and Charlotte insisted we use songs that pertained to the job. Right now, I wished I had a cool James Bond ringtone to go with my detective work.

"Emma Lee, I'm afraid the great beyond has paired me with someone who is never going to figure out what happened to me. Can't you worry about Zula after I find the light and head on over to the great beyond?" Ruthie stood up. A grimace of pain crossed her face. "Ouch," she groaned, reaching around and kneading her lower back.

"I'm doing the best I can." I opened the back door of the funeral home.

All the lights were out. I exhaled a thankful sigh that no one else had died. It wasn't like Sleepy Hollow had a death each week. It didn't, but when it rained it poured and Sleepy Hollow didn't need a flood.

She followed me into my office. I flipped on my light and pulled my notebook out of my purse.

"What kinds of questions do you have that might help find my killer?" Ruthie eased into one of the office chairs.

Even though the offices were located in the back of Eternal Slumber, I pulled the curtains closed so no one passing by would see me talking to myself.

I flipped my little detective notebook open. "How well do you know Hettie Bell?"

"Why?" Ruthie scooted to the edge of the chair, trying to get a peek of my notes. "What does she have to do with me?"

I tapped my notebook. "Why would she be seeing Doc Clyde? And why did she come to Sleepy Hollow of all places?"

Ruthie eased out of the chair and slowly paced back and forth. "I don't know much about her. We pay her barely over minimum wage. She did get mad at me for not letting her take off one day. I told her no but Zula told her yes."

I jotted down the day and made a note to ask Granny about it.

"Of course she went ahead and took the day off, leaving me shorthanded." Ruthie's eyes narrowed and she stared at me. "There is something different about her. She's not as tough as she wants everyone to think."

"Where was Granny the day Hettie asked off work?" The inn wasn't so busy that it couldn't be managed by one person.

"I have no idea. I'm not her keeper or her calendar." Ruthie slowly turned, her eyes were as big as saucers. She stuck her crooked finger in the air. "I just remembered seeing Zula coming out of the mayor's office that afternoon."

"Why would she be in the mayor's office?"

Ruthie winced and rubbed her back. "I have no idea. Can you look at my back?"

"Let me see." I walked over and flipped on the desk light. I tilted it toward Ruthie so I could get a good look at what was causing her pain. "It's weird that you can feel pain."

"It's not so much a pain, but an ache." She stood up and turned around slowly, lifting up the back of her hot-pink pajama top.

I twisted the light and squatted down to get a better view.

"It's a bruise." I dismissed the small black and purple circle that was no bigger than a dime and moved away.

"It's not just a bruise." Ruthie craned her neck and shifted her pajama top to see if she could get a look at it. "It hurts."

"Bruises hurt." I didn't see what the big deal was. Old people were always bruising themselves. "I'm sure it's from the fall. You did fall down a flight of stairs."

"How many times do I have to tell you that I didn't fall?" Ruthie mumbled. "I've been feeling it since the two hands pinched me and then pushed me."

"Wait!" I twirled my finger, signaling her to turn back around. "Let me see it again."

Ruthie stood and I placed both my hands on her back. The bruise was in a perfect place for a pinch from someone's right ring finger.

"Did it feel like your skin got pinched by a ring?" I pulled my hands away and then put them back.

"Maybe it was a ring." Ruthie agreed. Her voice escalated.

Did we have our first real clue? Excitement

boiled in me. I walked over to the closet in my office where I kept different suit jackets and a jewelry box for quick wardrobe change in case I needed one. I was notorious for spilling food on myself or a drip of coffee or two.

I grabbed a ring and put it on my right ring finger.

"Pull your shirt back up," I ordered her, and put my hands on the spot on her back. Ruthie's skin and pajama top were so thin, it would be easy to give her a little pinch.

I bent down and got real close. There seemed to be some sort of imprint on her skin where the small bruise was.

"Hold on." I took a closer look and outlined some indentions in the bruise. "Look."

Ruthie twisted and turned to try to get a look.

"What is that?" Ruthie questioned. "It looks like it branded me."

"It's some sort of imprint from the ring." I zeroed in on the small detail of a pointy-shaped thing and a hole. The hole looked like it should be filled.

I picked up my notebook. "I think we have our first real clue."

I jotted down my new discovery and drew a picture of what I had seen.

Chapter 9

Knock, Knock.

I jumped and looked around to find Vernon Baxter knocking on my office door. He was a stately older man I was sure was the cat's meow in his younger years. His salt-and-pepper—more salt than pepper—hair, along with his steel-blue eyes, made him look very old-Hollywood debonair.

"Hey, Vernon." I had completely forgotten Dr. Baxter was coming in to do the autopsy on Ruthie that Jack Henry had ordered. "You scared me."

Ruthie walked over to Vernon, big grin planted on her face. Her jewelry jingled when she reached out to touch him. He stepped forward, walking right through Ruthie. She looked down, almost disappointed that he didn't feel her.

She gathered her hands to her heart, sadness dripped on her face, she hung her head and disappeared.

Odd. I took in Ruthie's reaction when she saw Vernon. Quickly I jotted a V in my notebook to remind me to ask Ruthie about her reaction when she saw him.

"Sorry, Emma Lee." His blue lab coat made his hair look much grayer than normal. There was concern surrounding his eyes. "I'm a little shocked that Sheriff Ross is investigating Ruthie Sue's death as a murder."

"No stone unturned is what he said to me." I closed the notepad. The clock on the wall said I had fifteen minutes to get to the town council meeting and I didn't want to be late. The last thing I needed was to bring more attention to myself. Especially now that I was undercover.

I held Ruthie's file out for him to take. Now that the death was considered under investigation for a possible homicide, all the paperwork had to be changed. And the death certificate would take even longer to get. Like it or not, Ruthie was going to be here for some time.

"I hope they find out who did this." There was such a sincerity in Vernon's voice, it made my own heart ache. He took the file and opened up to the first page, where we always tape a living photo and death photo of the client. He stared at the page. "She was such a good woman."

Ruthie came back into the office. She looked like she had been crying. She stood on Vernon's right side with her hands, one over top the other, placed on her heart. Vernon bobbled his head to the right and looked at the empty space next to him as if he could feel that something or someone was there.

Many times during layouts at Eternal Slumber, family members would make the comment that they could feel their loved one there, but was Vernon that "close" to Ruthie to be able to feel her?

"Does he have any suspects?"

"I don't think so, at least I haven't heard of any. But I can't wait to see what you find out." I didn't let him know about the bruise or anything else that Ruthie told me. If he was a good coroner, he'd see it for himself. "I've got to go to the council meeting. I'll see you later."

I stuck my notebook in my purse. Vernon followed me out of the office and I locked it behind us.

"Vernon?" I stopped him from going back to the basement to work on Ruthie. I didn't want to pry, but I needed to know why Ruthie was so touched by seeing him and why her death was clearly affecting him the way it was.

"How well did you know Ruthie?"

The wrinkles around his eyes softened, almost dewy. "We had some social gathering, if you know what I mean." His brows lifted. "We old fogeys have to stick together."

Vernon walked me to the front door. Along the way I fluffed the floor-to-ceiling drapes that hung from the hallway of wooden encased windows, so they would bellow out on the bottom.

Eternal Slumber once was a beautiful old home, which Granny had restored.

"I'll let you know." Vernon held the door handle. "It could take weeks for some of the tests he's ordered to come back."

Ruthie stood between us. I tilted my head to the side so I could look at Vernon. Contrary to popular belief, ghosts weren't see-through. At least not Ruthie's.

"*Weeks?*" Ruthie stood outside when I opened the door to leave. "It's freezing in that cooler. Especially in this." She lifted up the edge of her pajama shirt.

"Thanks, Vernon." You'd think I was getting better at having two conversations, but I wasn't.

I heard him lock it when I made it to the other

side. Normally we didn't bother locking the funeral-home door during the day, but with a killer on the loose . . . no one was safe.

"We don't have weeks, Emma Lee." Ruthie was already sitting in the passenger seat of the hearse when I got in.

"We will talk later," I mumbled under my breath. Unfortunately, there was nothing I was able to do. A warrant was a warrant. Ruthie's body was in the hands of the law. "I'm on my way to the courthouse for the council meeting. Maybe the guy that was talking to the mayor at your layout will give us some insight to why someone might want to murder you with the proposal he is going to present at the meeting."

Ruthie didn't like my answer. Her arms were crossed, her face was stern and her eyes bored into me.

Chapter 10

There was silence as I drove slowly down the street in front of the courthouse to find a parking spot big enough for the hearse, but all the spots along the street were filled. Finally, I had to settle on a spot a couple of streets over. It would have been much easier to walk from Eternal Slumber, but I didn't know that everyone in the town was coming out to the meeting. Generally, no one showed up at these things.

I walked faster when I heard the courthouse clock chime five o'clock. My curiosity was killing me and I wanted to get a good seat, but by the looks of things, it was going to be standing room only.

I was right. The meeting room was filled to the gills. I inched my way to the back left corner.

I didn't see Ruthie, but that didn't mean she wasn't lingering around somewhere. In fact, I was sure she'd show up. Even though she was a ghost, she was just as nosy in the afterlife as she was in the living life.

Rolling up on my tiptoes, I could see Granny in the front row, along with a few other business owners, and Hettie.

Why were Granny and Hettie there? Who was at the inn? Not that Granny had to tell me her agenda, but she always did. Why was today any different?

Bang, bang, bang. Mayor May brought the gavel up and down. The sleeveless dress showed off her toned, tanned arms. Every woman in the room looked envious. Mayor May had no underarm skin flapping going on what-so-ever.

The mayor gave a little wink and wave to people greeting her.

I covered my mouth as I saw Ruthie appear behind the mayor and mock her every move. Ruthie had the wink and wave down to a tee.

"Did I tell you that she had been ignoring me up until my layout?" Ruthie yelled over the crowd.

I pretended not to hear or see Ruthie, but she

did do a good impression of the mayor, which brought a smile to my face.

"I'm bringing Sleepy Hollow council meeting to order." Mayor May smiled, Ruthie smiled, standing at the podium with the gavel haphazardly dangling from the tips of her bright red fingernails.

There should be a law against a mayor who was so pretty. Her fashion sense was the envy of every woman in Sleepy Hollow, including me. It was rumored that she had a stylist from Lexington that she secretly went to once a month.

Her red knee length dress fit her as if it was made just for her, giving a hint of her lean legs, which ended in five-inch heels.

"We are going to go over our regular agenda." The Mayor sashayed her way back to her seat, where she had the biggest name plate on the council. Never once did she bobble on those heels. Before sitting down, she said, "Then we will open the floor to any public discussions."

She ordered the treasurer to go over the budget, which took about ten minutes, followed by event planning and the usual items.

"Thank you." Mayor May nodded, Ruthie nodded, to the council members as each of them gave their monthly report. "Let's open up the floor to any business the community feels needs to be addressed."

"I'd like to address the good people of Sleepy Hollow." The gentleman from Ruthie's layout stood up and buttoned the middle button on his black suit coat.

"Please come forward." Mayor May pointed her gavel toward the podium at the front of the room. "You need to state your name clearly for the secretary."

Ruthie rushed next to the man's side.

The man followed her orders. He put his papers on the podium and adjusted the microphone. I dug into my purse and pulled out my notebook and pencil.

Ruthie read the papers over the man's shoulder and then looked up at me. It looked as if Ruthie's ghost had seen a ghost. She shook her head.

"I told them no, Emma Lee!" She shouted and pointed to the mayor and the other council members.

No, what?

"Scott Michaels." He spoke into the microphone and tilted his head toward the secretary. She was too busy to look at him as she continued to take the minutes from the meeting. "I'm with Grover and Grover Developers."

Developers? Suddenly I remembered Scott Michaels standing across the street from the inn with his fancy camera. *Oh no!*

I glanced over at Granny. She was sitting on the edge of her chair with her ankles crossed and hands planted firmly in her lap like a good Southern woman.

Was this why Granny updated the inn with more modern furniture? Did Granny know about this all along?

I jotted down everything Scott Michaels was saying. He went on and on about how building a five-star hotel would bring more tourists to Sleepy Hollow and the perfect spot was where Sleepy Hollow Inn was located because of the extra land and the easy route to the caves.

He had all sorts of papers with land plots, designs and a new logo for Sleepy Hollow. Things I didn't understand were in there.

"This is why she wouldn't see me when I went to talk to her." Ruthie stood nose to nose with Mayor May. "She went behind my back and made Zula a deal!"

Ruthie was on the verge of losing it. There was no way Granny would ever give up the inn to a big-time hotel chain. She loved Earl and the inn he gave her. She loved being there among the tourists and cooking for them. Granny loved to be known as the town's best hostess. She did it in the funeral business, she did it at the inn.

"We are in the early stages of talks with Mrs. Payne." He gestured toward Granny. Slightly she turned in her seat and nodded to the residents.

My mouth dropped. I couldn't believe my eyes. Had Granny known about this all along?

"I don't agree with this!" Hettie Bell jumped to her feet and stood up and pointed her finger directly at Granny. "Ruthie Sue Payne did not agree with this and now that she's dead, you think you can just sell the inn?"

Ruthie made her way over to Hettie and clapped her hands, giving Hettie a standing ovation. Her jewelry jangled louder and louder with each clap.

"That's right, Hettie Bell. You tell them," Ruthie said.

Too bad Hettie couldn't hear her or even the crowd that was getting rowdy.

Bang, bang, bang!

"Order!" Mayor May slammed the gavel so hard, the echo rang in my ears. "I'm going to have to ask you to leave, Ms. Bell, if you are not able to control yourself and act like a lady."

"What can we do as a community if we don't want a big hotel coming in here and destroying everything Sleepy Hollow stands for?" Hettie protested. If I didn't know better, I'd think Hettie had more at stake in Sleepy Hollow. But what? Why was so she concerned about what Sleepy Hollow stood for? She wasn't even from here.

There were a few more comments and concerns from the collective group.

"You can draw up a petition and have at least seventy-five percent of the community against the proposed hotel." Mayor May flipped her day planner and ran her finger down a page. "The petition needs to be filed in two days."

"Two days?" Hettie questioned. "That doesn't give me time to really make a campaign. Do you know anything about this Grover and Grover? Did any other company make offers? How do you know there isn't another site in Sleepy Hollow to develop?"

Hettie made some good points. I jotted each of them down.

"That's enough!" Mayor May stood up. Her eyes narrowed as much as her skirt. "Two days, Ms. Bell."

The crowd rumbled.

Bang, bang, bang.

Mayor May yelled above the chatter, "We will convene in two days to discuss any further plans with the development. Mr. Michaels is going to post the plans in the hallway for you to make a decision for yourself. If you want to sign a petition after you see the plans, find Ms. Bell." She smacked the gavel down. "This meeting is adjourned."

Everyone filed out one by one. I slipped outside without anyone seeing me.

"I can't believe you could do that to Ruthie when you knew she told the mayor she didn't want to sell." I couldn't see Hettie, but I could hear her.

I peeked around the side of the courthouse to see who she was yelling at. The shadow of the sinking sun hid my prying eyes.

"You know nothing about this," Granny hissed back at Hettie like a snake. "You are fired!"

Granny held her head up, straightened her back and walked down the sidewalk toward the inn.

"You know what," Hettie yelled after Granny, "I quit! It gives me more time to get a petition signed and stop this nonsense!"

"That, you need to check out." Suddenly, Ruthie stood behind me. Her eyes were as big as saucers.

Chapter 11

There was no way I was going to go and see Granny after all the commotion from the council meeting. She was fit to be tied as she stomped her way back to the inn after Hettie yelled back at her. Granny was too classy to even give Hettie a second glance, but I knew she was plotting her sweet revenge. And going to see her at this moment would only put me on her bad side, which was someplace I didn't want to be.

I needed to be on her good side so she would tell me the truth behind her rendezvous at midnight with Doc Clyde and her little conversations with the developer.

Stopping by Higher Grounds Café to enjoy a fresh cup of coffee might take just enough time and space from the meeting for me to go pay her a visit.

Anyway, it was almost six o'clock and Granny would have her hands too full at the inn with the supper crowd to be bothered with me.

The line was out the door and down the sidewalk at Higher Grounds. Walking past, I couldn't help but overhear a few hushed whispers about the meeting and the big news of a new developer in town. I made my way to the end of the line.

Hmm . . . maybe I could get some information that I didn't have if I went in, sat at the counter having one cup of coffee while "minding my own business," but keeping my ear close to the ground just in case.

"Shooo wee, I heard there was a little ruckus over at the council meeting tonight." Cheryl Lynne Doyle grabbed my arm. She pulled me out of the crowd and into the café. "I've got a table of one, just for you." She patted my arm in an empathetic way.

I wasn't sure if that was a dig to my single status, but I went anyway. Cheryl Lynne and I grew up together in Sleepy Hollow. It wasn't until high school that Cheryl Lynne blossomed and suddenly got very popular, leaving me in the dust, and I didn't mean cremation dust . . . social dust.

All the guys loved how Cheryl Lynne's Southern drawl was just that . . . *drawn out*. It was even prettier coming out of those perky red lips of hers. Cheryl Lynne was far from stupid even though she was the perfect stereotype of a blonde: petite, ample breasts and a perfect size six, without a single blemish . . . *ever*!

Cheryl Lynne had gone on a senior trip to New York City and when she discovered the fancy coffee houses, she knew that a coffee shop was exactly what Sleepy Hollow needed. And with the Doyle money, her daddy had no problem buying up the old post office building next to the courthouse to give Cheryl Lynne her own coffee house, Higher Grounds Café.

I followed her in, squeezing through the crowd. Most of the people I recognized from the council meeting, so I figured that everyone had gathered after the meeting to see what everyone else was thinking about the big news.

The café wasn't a large space and I was sure the fire department would be here any minute to shut the place down due to overcapacity.

"You sit," Cheryl Lynne ordered, pulling out the chair from the single-top half-moon-shaped table.

The crowd's whispers overlapped one another, each one debating the pros and the cons of a new five-star hotel coming to Sleepy Hollow. Of course most of the pros were the business owners of the community, while the cons were the residents who didn't want their small community taken over.

"Tell me all about the new developer," she squealed, and put the biggest coffee mug in front of me. I swear it was a watering trough and if I drank all the coffee she put in it, I'd be up all night looking for clues—or going to the bathroom.

"He wants to put a big hotel where the inn is." I picked up the cup, steadying it with both hands. The steam rolled up my nose. There was nothing that smelled or tasted better than a fresh cup of coffee.

"I swear, Emma Lee," Cheryl Lynne waved me off, "you are so funny. No wonder you are still single. I'm talking about his looks." Her eyes rose, the glitter on her lids glistened against the black mascara. She put up a finger when someone called for her. "Hold that thought."

The single-person table where Cheryl Lynne seated me was actually a great spot. It was positioned perfectly in the back with a full view of the café and all the other tables, which were filled, leaving most people to stand around discussing the issue at hand.

I got my notebook out of my purse and drew a map of the inside of the café, labeling the tables one through ten. Some were three toppers, while most were four.

Table one: Beulah and a few of the Auxiliary women.
Table two: Mary Anna and Ina Claire.

I glared at Ina Claire for a minute just to see if she could feel me. I was still mad at her for treating me like I was crazy. I reached in my purse and felt for Granny's file. If anyone did find out I stole it, I definitely could claim temporary insanity. I had plenty of witnesses at Doc Clyde's office, including Ina Claire and Hettie. Something told me that Ina Claire would be the first in line to tell them about my peculiar behavior.

I went back to observing the rest of the tables and jotting down who was sitting at them. Someone in here had to have known something having to do with the developer, Ruthie, or Hettie.

I inched my way up to table one, where Beulah Paige Bellefry was sitting. I pretended to look at the magazines Cheryl Lynne had hung on one of the old rungs from the slanted wooden ladder propped up against the wall that was used as a magazine rack.

Surely Beulah Paige had something worthwhile to say. Even if it wasn't a clue, she was still entertaining.

"I did hear that Ruthie Sue didn't want to sell it for any cheaper than two million dollars," Beulah whispered loud enough for everyone to hear. "But that was just some gossip, of course. God bless Ruthie's soul."

The other auxiliary women at the table nodded, bowed their heads, closed their eyes like they were God blessing Ruthie's soul.

Two million dollars? My mind couldn't even picture that kind of cash. What was Ruthie thinking?

"Did she ever find out about that picture she was researching?" One of the blue-haired ladies asked.

Picture? What picture? There were some things that Ruthie hadn't been forthcoming about and I needed her to tell me everything in order to help her figure out who murdered her.

Quickly Beulah Paige shushed her and looked at me. I reached for a *Cottage Today* magazine and flipped it open, pretending not to hear them.

Ears low to the ground. Too late . . .

"Good evening, Emma Lee." Beulah tossed her newly dyed red hair behind her shoulders. A new color choice for her.

"Good evening, ladies." I held the magazine up. "Thinking about doing some redecorating." I lied. I lied again, "I like your new hair color, Beulah."

I moved out of the way when a man with a guitar took a small rug and rolled it out over the top of my shoes.

"Excuse me." A little annoyed, I scooted my feet from under the rug.

"Can you please move somewhere else?" He jabbed his guitar at me. He pointed to the poster on the wall. "I'm the live entertainment tonight and this is my spot."

"Live music?" I read the poster. I had no idea Higher Grounds had live entertainment. "I'm so sorry." I shuffled to the side.

"Redecorating like your granny just did with the inn?" Beulah gave a crocked smile. I swear I saw devil horns pop out on each side of her flaming red head. "I bet Ruthie Sue Payne wasn't even cold when Zula Fae got rid of her stuff."

I ignored her. I knew she was baiting me.

"Don't you love what Granny has done to the place, though?" I asked.

"I do!" One of the other women at Beulah's table jumped right on in. "I went there for dinner with Ina Claire the other day, and Zula really does have the best fried chicken and sweet tea around."

The table rattled and the lady rubbed her shin. I was sure Beulah gave her a swift kick under the table—or poked her with her devil pitchfork.

"Have a nice evening, ladies." I smiled.

Beulah nodded her head. "Emma Lee?"

I cringed when I heard Beulah call me back.

"Yes, ma'am?" I used my good Southern manners and turned around. I clutched the magazine to my chest and tried to be the good woman my granny expected me to be.

She patted the empty chair at the four top that was right next to her. I sat down.

"Tell me." She leaned in, her blue eyes were like ice. "Why do they think Ruthie was killed?"

The other two women leaned in. I leaned back.

"I have no clue." I shrugged.

"Emma Lee, don't you be going around lying to us. We know that you and that . . ."

"Jack Henry," one of the other ladies finished her sentence.

"Jack Henry have a date tomorrow night." Beulah winked. "Surely he lets you in on all his little secrets."

I shook my head. "Who told you we have a date? Because we don't," I protested.

"Emma Lee," Beulah reached over and squeezed

my leg to the point where I grimaced. "You aren't trying to persuade him not to call Zula Fae a suspect with your . . ." she looked me up and down, sarcasm dripping from her lips " . . . *Southern charm, are you?*"

I jumped up and the chair crashed down behind me, smacking the floor. All the hushed gossip about the development had stopped.

"Beulah Paige Bellefry!" I pointed at her. "You should be the one in that casket, not Ruthie! Don't you dare go around accusing me of trying to persuade Jack Henry on this investigation! You will regret it!"

"She was acting this crazy at the office today," Ina Claire whispered.

I turned to glare at her, but realized the entire café was staring at me, even the guitar player, and the only sound was the percolating coffee coming from behind the counter.

"Emma Lee, darling, are you okay?" Cheryl Lynne stood by my single table with my purse in her hand. "Maybe you have had too much coffee."

"It's okay, Emma Lee." Mayor May stood in the door next to Scott Michaels. "It is very hard to adapt to changes." She winked and waved.

I grabbed my purse from Cheryl's grip and

marched past everyone and stopped at the mayor. It took everything I had not to reach out and grab those fake lashes off her eyes.

Instead, I turned back around, looked at the crowd and then zeroed in on the guitar player. "Start strumming!" I screamed before I dashed out the door, behind the courthouse and back into the safety of my hearse.

Chapter 12

A few minutes later, I had the hearse parked in the town square parking lot. The inn was packed. Maybe Sleepy Hollow needed another restaurant instead of a five-star hotel.

I stomped across the street, still mad at Beulah's comments on my real intentions for going on a date with Jack Henry. Though I couldn't dismiss that she might have a good point, which made me even more mad at myself for thinking that I'd use him to help Granny.

The concrete walkway, which Granny just had put in, was bordered with an assortment of spring flowers native to the region. Granny spent any and all free time working in the yard, which made me question why she'd consider selling the inn when she clearly loved it. She had put in such hard work.

The inn, positioned in a wooded area and tucked back into a cavern's hollow with the mountains as a backdrop, was a truly beautiful place to stay. No wonder it was the site the developer wanted.

When I walked in, Granny was busy serving a guest. I went back outside and planted myself in one of the rocking chairs to calm down. There was just something about that front porch that made my worries lessen. Plus, the cool night breeze might calm me down.

Beulah Paige did a good job making me and Granny look like fools in front of everyone. I hated myself for losing control. It only gave them ammunition that I was crazy and another reason for them *not* to use Eternal Slumber Funeral Home for their loved ones. I guess that was what I got for eavesdropping.

Sigh. I took a deep breath before I pulled the notepad out of my purse and jotted down what I did know. *Ruthie would sell the inn for two million dollars. Ruthie was trying to figure out who was in a picture. What picture?* Ruthie never made mention about a picture.

"Slow down." The rocker came to an abrupt halt

when Granny put her hand on the back. "You are shaking the entire inn. What is wrong with you?"

Granny wiped her hands off on her apron and sat in the rocker next to me.

"There's my brooch!" Ruthie plopped in the rocker next to Granny. Sure as I was sitting there, the spider brooch was pinned on the strap of Granny's apron.

Granny reached over and put her hand on mine. "Please tell me what's wrong. I'm so worried about you."

"That Beulah Paige Bellefry is a mean old lady and has the flaming red hair to prove it." Granny always told me to watch out for a red head with a hot temper. She should know since she and Charlotte both have red hair. I was going to wait to ask her about the brooch. If I even brought up Ruthie, I'm sure she'd make up an excuse to go inside. "I went into Higher Grounds Café to get a coffee and almost every single citizen was in there talking about the council meeting."

I paused and waited to see if Granny was going to spill her guts about the developer, but she only gestured me to go on.

"Beulah is hardly old," Granny reminded me. "If forty-two is old, I'm ancient."

Ruthie reached out and tried to snatch the brooch, only to come up short.

"You better get my brooch back and stick it on me in that freezer!" Ruthie continued to eyeball Granny, while I continued to ignore her.

"Whatever." I waved my hand, trying to get Ruthie to go away, and focused on Granny. "Anyway, Beulah hinted around that I was only going out with Jack Henry to persuade him not to arrest you for Ruthie's murder." That should get her attention.

She clasped her hands and squealed, "You are going out with Jack Henry?"

My mouth dropped open and my eyebrows swooped downward. "Granny, did you hear me?"

"No she didn't hear you." Ruthie's cheeks were balled up with red dots. "She's a senile old lady that stole my brooch. Ask her. See if she goes to twitching." Ruthie got up and hopped around on her kitty slippers, twitching her eyes, doing her best imitation of Granny.

I twisted my body to focus more on Granny.

"Yes. You have a date with Jack Henry and I can't believe you didn't tell me." Granny had been on a mission for years to get me hooked up with Sleepy Hollows' most eligible bachelor. "That boy comes from good stock."

"No, the part about you killing Ruthie." I stood up and paced the veranda. "Everyone in town thinks that you killed her."

"Emma Lee, why on earth would I kill Ruthie?" She cackled as if it was a farfetched idea.

"Well . . ." I crossed my arms and tapped my shoe, "for starters, you two hated each other and . . ."

"That's nonsense," Granny interrupted and protested as she looked the other way. "Hate is a strong word for a Southern woman to have in her vocabulary, much less use. You must watch what you say and how you say things, Emma Lee."

I ignored her and continued, "And she didn't want to sell the inn and you do!" I pointed at her. There. She had to tell me about the developer *now*. "When were you going to let me in on the whole new development thing?"

"When there was something to tell."

"And having a council meeting based around this wasn't enough 'something' to tell?" I made sure to make the air quotes in the air. Granny always hated them. She said that you should never talk with your hands unless you needed to use sign language.

"Emma Lee, you have enough on your plate to worry about this old inn."

"And the brooch." I pointed to the ugly-looking spider. "That was Ruthie's."

Granny hid the brooch with her hand; her mouth dropped open. She gasped, "How did you know about this brooch?"

"It was in Ruthie's pre-arrangements." I raised an eyebrow. "You should know better than anyone that the client always lists what they want to be buried with." I reached over and tapped the top of her hand that was still covering the ugly pin. "And that was on her list."

A guilty look flushed her cheeks. She batted her lashes. "Earl wanted me to have it."

Ruthie and I both waited for the twitch.

"How did she know I kept it in my shoe box under the pillows in my closet?" Ruthie begged to know.

"How did you know it was under all of those pillows if you didn't go through Ruthie's things?" I asked.

"Emma Lee, first off, I don't like you accusing me of stealing something that was given to me by my late husband." She cast down her eyes. I flickered remembering her words about hot-tempered, redheaded women. "Secondly, how did *you* know it was in the closet under the pillows?"

"Ah, oh." Ruthie pulled back and looked at me.

"It was in her arrangement packet on where I could find it." I lied . . . yet again.

"Good!" Ruthie nodded her head in delight.

"Earl told me." Lightly, Granny brushed her fingers across it like it was a pet spider instead of a brooch. "He told me that when Ruthie died, I was to keep the brooch."

"Liar!" Ruthie stomped around the front porch.

Granny wasn't lying. Her eyes were as calm as a baby with its belly full. No twitching whatsoever.

"What about Hettie?" I threw my hands in the air, giving up on the whole brooch thing. As far as I was concerned, Ruthie had her explanation. Besides, she couldn't take it with her to the other side, but somehow I knew Earl was going to hear about it once she got ahold of him in the great beyond. "They were talking about you firing her and her quitting. What is that about?" I lied about overhearing someone. I bet if I would've kept my big mouth shut at the café, I'd have heard something about the fight.

"Obviously she was sticking her nose in some business she had no business sticking her nose in." Granny was good with words and switching them around to confuse me. "It's time for dessert." She got out of the rocker. "You can either help me or go home."

She walked in, the screen door slamming behind her.

Like a good granddaughter, I went in to help. After all, Hettie wasn't there and I knew she always helped wash the dishes after the supper crowd.

Chapter 13

I didn't know much about ghosts, but I was sure Ruthie Sue Payne was avoiding me. Ever since last night and the debacle with Beulah, and finding out that Earl had broken her trust and told Granny exactly where she kept the spider brooch he had given her, Ruthie hadn't shown up. Even when I called out for her.

Good news was that I got some sleep and knew the first thing I needed to do this morning was apologize to Cheryl Lynne Doyle for making a scene at her café last night.

After taking a quick shower and throwing on a pair of jeans and a T-shirt, I took advantage of the beautiful spring morning and decided to walk to Higher Grounds.

The town square was already buzzing with runners, walkers and gathered groups drinking coffee. Colorful flower baskets hung from the carriage lights lining the sidewalk around the square.

I loved this time of the year, especially when the weather was this nice. Stopping for a brief moment, I bent down to smell the flowers in the decorative urn that was on the sidewalk across the street from Higher Grounds Café. Although, I was admiring the beautiful flowers, I was really building up my self-confidence to go in and apologize for being . . . crazy.

I wished I could be like the black-eyed Susan and bask in the morning sun, but it was time to face the music.

A few seconds later, I was across the street and walking in Higher Grounds. The smell circled my nose, making my taste buds water.

"Good morning." I greeted Cheryl Lynne.

"Emma Lee, we don't want any trouble this morning." Cheryl wiped her hands off on her apron and walked around from behind the counter. Her blond hair was pulled into a high ponytail, causing her eyes to become taut at the ends and slant upward.

Three of the tables were filled with customers. Of course, Beulah Paige Bellefry was one of them. Just my luck.

Inwardly I groaned, but put a sweet smile on my face. "Morning, Beulah." It actually pained me to say her name. *Kill them with kindness*, Granny would say. "Cheryl, I'm so sorry for what happened last night. I'm here to apologize. I was only trying to defend my *granny*." I turned and glared at Beulah, who had an ear turned in my direction, and then I turned back to talk to Cheryl.

"Fine." Cheryl patted my arm. "We Southern women sure do love our family." She smiled, giving me the signal that she'd be sure to spread the word. "Let me get you a cup of coffee."

The glass-covered platters sitting along the counter were filled with delicious-looking homemade scones, muffins and doughnuts. Each one looked better than the next.

"Who makes all of your pastries?" My mouth watered.

"I do." Cheryl's voice escalated with pride. "I get up every morning at three A.M. to start baking. I love it." She looked beyond my shoulder.

"I had no idea you were a baker." My eyes were bigger than my stomach.

I couldn't decide, looking down the line of goodies. There were long johns, apple fritters, all sorts of scones, cinnamon buns, chocolate doughnuts, some with sprinkles, and a lot of bagels.

I turned around when someone cleared their throat. Vernon Baxter was patiently waiting behind me. I stepped aside.

"I'll take two of those blueberry scones." Vernon nodded. "Morning, Emma Lee. I should have that report wrapped up soon."

"Thanks," I whispered. There was no way I wanted Beulah to know any more than she needed to know.

"Here you go, Dr. Baxter." Cheryl sat his bag of scones and my to-go cup on top of the counter and winked.

He tipped his head to me. "I'm on my way to the funeral home. Is Charlotte there to let me in?"

I checked the clock above the counter. "Nine o'clock, she better be there," I teased.

Of course she was there. Charlotte was never late for anything a day in her life, especially work. I sort of wished she wasn't there because I was sure she had already heard about last night's incident between me and old Beulah.

Thinking about it made me turn around and give Beulah one more good stare.

"See you soon." Vernon grabbed his bag of scones and headed on out.

"You know, Granny needs to hire you to make pastries for the inn." I picked up the lid to one of the glass platters and chose a cake doughnut.

"Ruthie and I were already in talks." Cheryl put the pastry in a bag and handed it to me. "I'm assuming Zula isn't interested since she wants to sell the place." Cheryl shrugged.

"We'll see about that." I plucked the bag from her fingers and thanked her. "On second thought, I'll take a couple of those scones that Vernon got."

Cheryl hurried up and bagged them because there was a line forming behind me. I'm sure the crowd came from across the street (the town square) where the scent was sure to float.

"See you soon." Cheryl handed me another bag.

"See ya." I wiggled my fingers. I thought about apologizing one more time, but once was probably enough.

"Poor Vernon," Beulah said as I walked by, just loud enough for me to hear. "He sure was in love with Ruthie. Especially since they were dating."

"I hope you are doing well this morning, Emma

Lee." Mayor May held the door open for me, winked and waved all at once.

Inwardly, I cringed at her talent of making everyone like her.

"Mayor, I'm so sorry for my behavior. It was very uncalled for, not to mention unprofessional." I was so glad to run into her. She and Charlotte were always talking about how important it was for business to be involved in the community. Maybe my little apology would stop the mayor from telling Charlotte about last night.

"Oh, don't worry." She brushed it off. "We all have bad days, don't we?"

"Yes we do." It was better to leave it at that instead of respond with a big reason for why I did fly off the handle. Granny always said, the less said, the better. I had made my peace and I wasn't going to bring it up again.

Even though I apologized to the right people, it was apparent that Beulah was intending to spread gossip about Vernon Baxter and Ruthie.

Which probably wasn't too far from the truth. I recalled Ruthie's reaction when Vernon had come into my office to get Ruthie's file for her autopsy. I recalled him saying that he did spend some time with Ruthie . . . socially.

Vernon was retired, but kept his license current by doing what few autopsies Eternal Slumber had, which wasn't many, per year.

Vernon and Ruthie a couple? I couldn't picture it. *Where was she anyway?*

It was too nice to go back to the funeral home and I had a bag full of blueberry scones. I looked right, down the sidewalk, and decided to walk to the Sleepy Hollow Inn, hoping it was a good time to question Granny with the temptation of a pastry.

Plus, we didn't get to finish our conversation about the developer and what her real plans were. Eternal Slumber didn't have a body, so there was no rush to get back.

"Mornin,' Emma Lee." John Howard nodded as I walked up to him. He was bent down on the sidewalk, hand picking out the wild weeds from the cement cracks.

He grumbled something about the weeds and how the mayor had asked him to help beautify the sidewalks, with the impending development, and then he threw his hands up in the air.

"Are you okay, John Howard?" I questioned. Frustration settled in his tense jaw.

"No, ma'am." He flicked his gaze at me. "I'm tired of putting in odd jobs all over the community in order to feed myself. O'Dell Burns offered me a full-time job doing his odd jobs around Burns Funeral Home." He stood up and shuffled his feet. He put his dirt-stained hands in his jeans pockets. "I hate to do it, but going to be giving my two-week notice. Two weeks is all I have to give, according to O'Dell."

"I'm sure the mayor will understand." I had heard that the mayor came up with some odd jobs when John Howard came to her and asked for work.

"I mean two weeks at Eternal Slumber."

Drawing in a deep breath, I said, "Oh. I . . . I see."

How could he? Anger swelled inside me. After everything Granny had done for him and he pays us back by leaving when times get tough?

"It's just that no one wants to use Eternal Slumber since . . . since . . ." He beat around the bush.

"Since I came down with the 'Funeral Trauma.'" I took the words right out of his mouth.

He shuffled faster, so much so that I thought he was going to be a human street sweeper.

"Fine." I let him off the hook. "I'll let Charlotte know."

I could beg him to stay with us and assure him that business was going to turn around, but the hard fact was that it wasn't. At least not until I could prove Granny didn't kill Ruthie and that I wasn't crazy.

Secretly, I thanked every single weed I saw in the sidewalk cracks on my way to the inn, because that meant John Howard had to bend over and pick each and every one of them.

Chapter 14

I found Granny in the kitchen cleaning up the last few plates from breakfast. I sat the bag on the table.

"Good morning." I walked over and gave Granny a kiss on the cheek.

"How is my Emma Lee this morning?" Granny held me at arm's length to get a good look. She stared into my eyes to see if she saw any crazy.

"I'm fine. *Great* morning." I pulled away. "John Howard gave his notice. He said Burns gave him a full-time job."

"That O'Dell Burns." Granny threw her towel into the sink, causing it to smack. She grumbled, "I never trusted that man."

"Luckily, we don't have a lot of business, so he did me a favor by not having to lay him off."

We sat in silence for a few seconds soaking in the news. I think we were both stunned since we had given John Howard everything he needed. We both knew that even if we didn't have any bodies for a long time, I would've never laid him off. There was always something for him to do around Eternal Slumber.

I changed the subject to a more pleasant topic: Cheryl's delicious pastries.

"Have you tried Cheryl Lynne's scones?" I pushed the bag toward Granny.

"I have." Granny took the bag and opened it. "They are delicious."

Granny halved one of the scones and gave me a half.

"Mmm . . ." Granny's eyes closed as she savored the other.

"You should buy some for the inn." I took my half and dunked it in the coffee.

"We shall see." Granny went back to the sink. She threw me a towel, which meant for me to get off my butt and help.

"Granny, please tell me about the developer." I dried each plate carefully. Granny never liked spots to be left on any dish.

"There is really nothing to tell." She took the plate and placed it in the rack that hung on the wall. "Mayor May introduced him to me. I told Ruthie about it and she protested only because it was the last little bit of Earl that was left for her to hang on to."

I let Granny talk, but that didn't make sense. Especially if Ruthie was seeing Vernon Baxter.

"Why would you sell? You love this place," I said.

"I'm getting older." She put the towel on the counter and leaned up against it. "Earl didn't want to be tied to this place in our later years. Plus it is a great growth opportunity for Sleepy Hollow."

Everything Granny said made sense.

"But it's a staple in the community." I picked up the last plate to dry. "Isn't there another piece of property somewhere else they can use?"

"No." Granny took the last dish, placed it in the rack and wiped down the counter. "Where the inn sits is the only real stable land that won't disturb the structure of the caves. I'm not saying I'm going to do it, but I'm not promising I won't."

There was some commotion going on in the hallway. I walked out of the kitchen with Granny following me. Suddenly I realized I was the only one who could see what all the fuss was about.

"My picture! You got my picture!" Ruthie was in the foyer looking at the ugliest framed photograph I had ever seen leaning up against the wall. She bounced up and down with delight.

"Emma Lee," Granny gasped. "Did you go up in the attic and get that gawd-awful picture out?"

"No." With my eyes wide open, I protested. "I've never seen it before in my life."

"I wonder who was snooping in my attic?" Granny walked down the hall and looked in each room. She was sure there was an intruder. "Take it back up to the attic. I have people coming here and I don't want anyone to see what this place used to look like."

Was this the picture that Beulah's friend had mentioned at Higher Grounds Café? Granny wasn't the one I needed to question, Ruthie was. If I took it to the attic like Granny told me to, I'd get Ruthie alone and question why she'd been researching it.

"No! Don't you dare put that away," Ruthie ordered and stomped her kitty-slippered feet up the steps right beside me. "If there is one thing that I want, it's that picture."

I ignored her until we were up the stairs, down the hall and next to the door that led to the scary attic.

"Where have you been?" I asked in a very hushed whisper. I sat the photo down. "I need to ask you all sorts of questions. You won't believe what has been going on around here."

"Like what?"

"Beulah Paige and I had a very public fight because she is spreading gossip about why I'm going out with Jack Henry tonight." *Amazing Grace*, my phone sang. I pulled it out to check what was on the agenda. I almost forgot that I had a hair appointment at noon. I put the phone back in my pocket. "You wanted two million dollars to sell this place and why do you want this photograph so badly?" I picked it up and shoved it in her face.

"Calm down, Emma Lee." Ruthie put her hands out to dampen my temper.

We both turned when we heard footsteps coming up the stairs. I opened the door to the attic and we walked up slowly, and in the dark.

"I hate this attic," I growled and knocked something with my feet. I pulled the cell back out of my pocket and used the flashlight app to offer some light.

There was an old box that was partially hidden under one of the floorboards that caught my attention.

I sat the picture back down and pulled the tin

box out. It looked like an old safety deposit box.

"Two million was to throw Zula off because I know this place isn't even worth a million. I had no idea Zula had gone as far as to call a developer." She rubbed her chin. "I had bigger issues to worry about. I think I might have a next of kin that is hidden in that picture." Ruthie's words sent chills up my spine. She pressed her nose up to the glass surface, and took her time looking at each person in the photo.

"What?" This could be the biggest news since her death was claimed a murder, and another clue. "These people look poor, and you are far from poor."

I held the phone flashlight up to the image so I could see better. There were six smiling people in the photo. Each one was wearing bibbed overalls. They weren't the cleanest bunch I'd ever seen. It didn't look like they had used water or gone to the dentist . . . *ever*.

"Family is family," Ruthie spouted. "I'm not sure, but I found this old picture at an estate sale a few months back and it spoke to me."

"Spoke to you?" Who was the crazy one here? "That's it." I grabbed the picture and was going to put it in an empty spot when she stopped me.

"Please, Emma Lee," Ruthie begged. "It's something. I just don't know what."

I picked up the old box from underneath the floorboard.

"Please." Ruthie was almost in tears. "Just try to check it out. What do we have to lose?"

I didn't know if I felt sorry for her or if something really was telling me to listen to her, but I took a chance. One problem, I had no clue how to find out who these people were.

"All right." I put the framed photo under one arm and the box under the other. "Let's get out of here without Granny seeing us . . . er . . me taking these."

Ruthie's smile was as long as the old country road that leads all the way down to the Kentucky River.

I eased down the steps, trying not to let them groan under me, and slowly opened the door. The coast was clear. We made it down the steps without seeing Granny.

I turned when I heard voices coming from the front snack room and peeked my head around the corner. Granny and Scott Michaels had their backs to me, with Mayor May looking over their shoulders.

Mayor May and I made brief eye contact before she winked and waved.

I jerked back.

Please don't mention last night, again. I prayed that Mayor May would let my apology ride and not worry Granny with my behavior.

I rushed out before anyone else saw me.

Chapter 15

A few minutes later, I and my little stash from Granny's attic were in the hearse and pulling up to the funeral home. I had to get the loot in before anyone saw me, but it was too late.

"Good afternoon." Jack Henry pulled up behind the hearse in his police cruiser.

When our eyes met, his smile widened, his teeth strikingly white against his handsome face. Every single part of me tingled. I gripped the picture frame in fear I would get weak in the knees.

"Hi, Jack Henry." I waved and reached back in the hearse to get the picture and box. I sat them against the car and slammed the door shut before walking over to his car.

I gulped, trying not to give any inclination that

my heart sank to my stomach when Jack Henry's familiar scent trickled up my nose. Every part of him was amazing and every woman knew it, including me.

"What in the world do you have there, Emma Lee?" I followed his finger to the picture.

For an instant I wondered if Ruthie hadn't died and he didn't need me for the investigation would he have still asked me out or taken the time to pull his car behind mine. I shook the thought out of my head. Of course he wouldn't have asked me out. "I . . . I got this stuff that might be some clues from Granny's attic."

"Is that right?" He looked between the two, unimpressed. "We need to discuss that whole situation over dinner tonight."

"I thought it was just karaoke." I lifted a brow, leaving me once again with the thought that he might, just might have a little inkling of feelings for me.

"It was, until it got all over town that you were going to woo me to let Zula off the hook." He flashed an evil grin.

"I see Beulah Paige Bellefry's rude comment got back to you." I propped myself up on my elbows on the rolled-down window to get a better look at him in his uniform, which made me inwardly swoon. "I can't believe her. If they only knew we were working on finding the killer to keep them safe."

"Darn." Jack Henry smacked his hands together. "I was prepared to be wooed."

"You go on, Jack Henry." I shooed him away and stepped back from the car. "You go arrest somebody until you pick me up at five thirty for dinner."

"It's a date." He pulled the gear shift down and took off.

The date was going to be either glorious or a disaster. He was playing it way too cool that I was able to see Ruthie and that I was trying to figure out who killed her. I knew I was going to have to play my cards right. And getting to the salon on time was exactly my first step in doing so. I had to look perfect.

I turned and headed up the funeral-home steps.

Chapter 16

I was right, Charlotte was working away on some-thing, which made it easy for me to slip into my office and store the picture and box.

I sat the picture down. Opening the office cur-tains, I let the sun trickle in, resting its light on the image. I backed away to get a better look—after all, I had only gotten a glance at it in the hallway and the lighting in the attic wasn't good since it was provided by my cell phone.

"Eww." I shivered. "It's even uglier in the direct light."

Ruthie was insistent that these six faces star-ing back at me had some sort of significance to her life. But did it have anything to do with her murder?

I couldn't help but wonder if I was going to be wasting my time trying to find out exactly how Ruthie was tied to the photograph—but anything to help Granny off the suspect list wasn't a waste of time.

Charlotte's heels clicking down the hardwood-floored hall between our offices caught my ear.

Quickly I shoved the items in the corner of the office closet and drew the curtains closed. The last thing I needed was Charlotte questioning me on what it was and where I had gotten it.

"Emma Lee, what is all this talk about Granny selling the inn to a developer?" Charlotte sashayed into my office. She put her hand on the door and leaned on it. Her long red hair was straight as a pine needle this morning, which made me envious. She managed to fix her hair in all sorts of styles, looking fabulous in each one.

"I don't know." I shut the closet door. "I asked her about it this morning and she blew me off. You should go ask her."

Granny and Charlotte had a different bond than me and Granny. Charlotte was a lot like Granny in the business world and dealing with people. Very poised, well-mannered and good with numbers. Me, I was the one who was good with details, making sure things got crossed off the funeral lists, which made Charlotte and me a perfect tag team for Eternal Slumber . . . until the "Funeral Trauma."

"And I heard Granny is a suspect in Ruthie's death." Charlotte eyed me. She was always good at getting me to talk.

"She didn't kill Ruthie." I rolled my eyes. I swear, the idle gossip in this town killed me. I straightened up the files on my desk by putting them in a pile. Charlotte hated it when my desk was a complete mess. And the top of the desk wasn't visible.

"I was murdered." Ruthie plopped herself on the newly clean spot on top of my desk with her legs dangling, kitty-slipper eyes rotating to the left and right from her shaking her feet. She zeroed in on Charlotte and said, "Tell Miss Hoity-Toity I was murdered."

"Maybe you should spend some more time with Granny instead of wasting all of your time in that office of yours." I held a couple of files tight to my chest and I ignored Ruthie and tried to focus on Charlotte. It was true. Charlotte spent so much time at work, and with no dead bodies, I was beginning to think she was the crazy one.

"I would if I didn't have to worry about all the back taxes Granny didn't pay." Charlotte's delivery of the news was as cold as one of our clients.

"What?" The files dropped from my hands, scattering all over the floor.

"She left us with a mess. And I'm sure Mom and Dad know nothing about it." Charlotte slowly shook her head. Disappointment hung in the air. "Those two men that were in here, they are from the IRS. Granny owes a lot of back taxes on the funeral home. A lot of money. I'm working with a big accounting firm out of Lexington to try to straighten the mess out."

Was that why Granny was so desperate to sell the inn? For a split second, I lost my mind and wondered if Granny killed Ruthie since Ruthie wouldn't sell her half of the inn. *But the twitch.*

"Yea, well I'm staying away from Granny until I get this fixed." Charlotte turned around, stopped, and then turned back to face me. "Listen, Granny is going to jail for either murder or fraud, unless we can figure this thing out."

My mouth dropped open. I couldn't say a word. How could Charlotte be so cold? There had to be an explanation. I turned to say something to Ruthie, but she was just as flabbergasted as I was.

"Do you think Granny did either of those things?" I asked Ruthie when Charlotte's office door clicked closed. It was so out of Granny's character, but a lot of things lately had been out of Granny's character.

"I don't know, Emma Lee." Sadness formed in the creases of Ruthie's eyes, proceeding to her turned-down mouth.

I was beginning to wonder if I knew Granny at all.

Chapter 17

No matter what was going on with the taxes, I was still on a mission to prove Granny didn't kill Ruthie and to go on my date with Jack Henry.

The pink awning over the windows of Girl's Best Friend Spa flapped in the spring breeze. The bell over the door sang "Diamonds Are a Girl's Best Friend" when I walked in. The spa was packed.

"It's a beautiful day," Mary Anna chirped and swiveled the chair of a customer she was working on. The customer didn't take a breath when Mary Anna greeted me as she continued to tell Mary Anna her story. I was sure it was some sort of gossip.

"It sure is." I muttered. Mary Anna had already

returned to the conversation she was having with her client.

I looked around at the eight stations that were filled with all sorts of hair products. I had no clue what any of them were used for.

Hair dryers and flat irons of all shapes and sizes dangled off hooks. Different styles of brushes were neatly displayed on top of each station along with multiple bottles of hair sprays and gels.

"You can help yourself to an afternoon cookie and coffee if you want to, Emma Lee." Mary Anna pointed the comb that was in her hand over to the waiting area.

I sat down on one of the two pink love seats that were positioned at the front of the store, right across from Mary Anna's homage to Marilyn Monroe. A huge portrait of Marilyn dripping in diamonds, her mouth spread open into a breathy grin, stared at me. The table underneath her had candles lit in her honor, along with a plateful of cookies.

The sun felt good shining through, almost warming my worried soul. There had been a ton on my mind before, but more now that Granny would have had a bigger motive to kill Ruthie. *Money.*

Patiently I waited until it was my turn, going

over all the clues in my head. Every single one of them pointed to Granny.

"All done!" One of the hairdressers swiveled her client around and caught my attention from the excitement in her voice. "You look fabulous!"

No! I squinted when I thought I recognized the person. *It can't be.*

It was.

Hettie Bell had gone from mousey to glamorous right before the hairdresser's eyes.

"Hi, Emma Lee." Hettie's long black hair was cut into a chin-length bob with blunt bangs hitting right above her brows.

"Hettie," I gasped. "You look great."

"I thought it was time for a change." She took out her wallet and paid the stylist. "Especially since I'm going to be in the public eye getting my little petition signed." She dangled a very official-looking document between her newly manicured light pink nails. She looked 180 degrees different from this time yesterday. "Would you like to sign it?"

"No thank you." I stood up when she approached, suddenly realizing she was much taller than me.

"You need to make sure you put this in your hair when it's wet." The stylist gave Hettie a hot pink bottle with the word TAME written in gold glitter across it. "This will take out that tight natural curl your hair has and make it easier to straighten."

I scanned the rest of the new Hettie Bell as she stood there taking in the instructions on how to get the perfectly styled hair the stylist had created. She wore a short white skirt with big blue flowers on it and a tank top under a jean jacket.

"It was good seeing you anyway." She waved the big pink bottle in the air; a big flower ring on her right ring finger caught my attention. "And tell that granny of yours that I'm going to get those signatures."

Hettie threw the product in her purse. She didn't give me time to say anything. She was out the door and already had someone stopped on the sidewalk signing the petition.

"That girl is on a mission." Mary Anna tapped me on the shoulder. "Come on. I've been dying to get ahold of that pretty little head of yours."

I can't say that I was totally transformed like Hettie Bell, but Mary Anna did the best she could with what she had to work with.

There were just enough caramel highlights for someone to think that I had just gotten back from the beach and just enough bounce to think I had had a great time while I was there.

"No big bangs?" Mary Anna twirled me around to the mirror for a final look.

"No." Playfully, I shook my head to see how it felt. "I do love it. You were right."

"I always am." She winked. "This one is on me."

"No!" I protested. "I can't let you do that."

"Honey, from what I hear, you need to save your money to get your granny off the hook with her tax evasion." She used her scissors to clip off any last stray hairs dangling from my new layers.

"How did you hear about that?"

"You stay around here long enough, and you will hear a lot of things." She waved the scissors in the air. "Right ladies?"

The other stylists laughed and agreed.

"Which reminds me . . ." Mary Anna paused, swiveled me around and looked me in the eyes. "I hear you have a date with hunky Sheriff Ross." She winked, twirling my chair back to face the mirror.

Beulah.

"I'm not even going to ask where you heard that from." I smiled, playing coy. If everyone in town wanted to think that Jack Henry asked me out because he wanted a date, it was fine with me. But Jack Henry and I knew why he asked me out.

One, to throw Charlotte off the day he was there questioning me about Ruthie. Two, because he needed me to talk to Ruthie's ghost to help solve her murder.

"Let me tell you, honey." Mary Anna was as breathy as Marilyn. She waved the comb in the air. "Just like Marilyn said, a career is wonderful, but you can't curl up with it on a cold night. And it gets pretty chilly around here, if you know what I mean."

I knew exactly what she meant.

"Here comes your favorite weekly appointment." One of the hairdressers nodded toward the door.

Mayor May was standing outside talking on her cell phone. She looked like Barbie with those long legs, short skirt suit and long hair cascading down her back.

"You do the mayor's hair?" I was impressed.

"If you only knew how long it took me to straighten that mess of curls." Mary Anna's lips pursed. She grabbed the can of hairspray. Using her hand to cover my eyes, she sprayed the sticky stuff all over my hair. "Every week I have to shampoo and straighten it. But she sure does look good after."

About that same time, the mayor rushed in.

"You aren't going to believe it!" She threw her hands in the air and left them hanging in the sky. And we all knew what that meant. A good Southern woman throws her hands up in the air to give thanks for something really big. "The big guys in Frankfort want me to run for governor! Can you believe it?" She planted her hands on her chest. "Little ol' me, mayor of Sleepy Hollow, the next governor of Kentucky?"

"Then we better get your hair done!" Mary Anna forgot all about me.

Everyone rushed over to congratulate her, everyone but me. Ruthie was right. Mayor May's actions at Ruthie's layout were all an act to get to the next election.

While everyone was taking their turn to congratulate her, it was my chance to slip out of there. I didn't want the mayor to question me about the scandal with the tax evasion at the funeral home.

If it was true and Granny hadn't paid her taxes, couldn't they just take the inn from her for the payment?

Out on the sidewalk I stepped to the side and pulled out my notebook. That was a good question to ask Jack Henry tonight at dinner. And I noted that Hettie was wearing a ring.

Chapter 18

The rest of the afternoon flew by until it was time to get ready for my dinner date . . . I used the word *date* loosely.

Blessed Assurance, my phoned chimed when a text came across.

> Mary Anna: Wear heels!
> Me: Ouch!
> Mary Anna: As Marilyn says, I don't know who invented high heels, but all women owe him a lot! Wear heels!
> Me: OK!

There was only one problem. The only good pair of heels, and I mean high heels, were the red ones I bought in Lexington a year ago when I was there for a convention. I had spent all of my money on them. I'd only worn them around my small efficiency apartment.

When Charlotte and I took over the funeral home, we turned our parents' residence into a larger gathering space for the families and friends of our clients. That was when Eternal Slumber got all the business . . . before I got the "Funeral Trauma."

Anyway, Charlotte wanted her own place to live and I was comfortable at the funeral home, so we made a little apartment in the back for me complete with a bedroom, kitchenette, bathroom and small television room. It was plenty enough for me.

It didn't take me long to thumb through my assortment of clothes in my closet.

"Boring." I looked at the blue skirt suit hanging up and scooted the hangers over until I got to the black suit. "Even more boring."

I took out the black-and-white pin-striped short skirt. I took it to the mirror that hung on the hallway wall and held it up to me.

"That one." Ruthie appeared over my shoulder. "You wear that with that white ruffled blouse, chunky necklace and fabulous red high heels."

"How do you know about my heels?" I questioned her. No one knew about my heels . . . or so I thought.

"I just so happened to be in Lexington the same time you were. I hid behind another shoe rack when I saw you trying them on." She smiled. "*Oh la-la!* was my exact thought when I saw how you looked in them. You had the brightest smile on your face."

"Really?" I could remember exactly how I felt that day I tried them on. "Then why didn't anyone else ask me about them?"

Unfortunately, living Ruthie would have told the world as soon as she got back into Sleepy Hollow.

"I can keep a secret if I need to." She shooed me with her hands. "Hurry up and get ready."

I smiled and did as she told me. I was beginning to regret that I didn't know Ruthie while she was alive. She was much more different than anyone knew.

Excitement twirled in my chest as I put on each piece of clothing. I came out a few minutes later to show her the finished product.

"No, no, no." Ruthie shook her head. She walked over and unbuttoned the top three buttons. "There." She fanned the blouse open. My collarbones and necklace were on display for the entire world to see. "Dare to be different."

"I don't want to be seen as . . . loose." I looked in the mirror.

"Listen." She put her hands on each of my shoulders as we both looked into the mirror. "If Jack Henry wanted a librarian, he'd have asked out the boring one at the Sleepy Hollow branch, but he didn't. He asked you out."

"You forget." I reminded her. "This is not a real date."

The knock at the door made my heart fall straight down into my toes, like a roller coaster. Ruthie was gone.

After one more quick look in the mirror, I opened the door.

"Wow." Jack Henry's mouth fell open. His eyes sparkled. "You look amazing."

"Thank you." I smiled and stepped out the door. I made sure I locked it before we headed out to his car.

"I'm sorry you have to be seen in the cruiser." He pointed to the Sleepy Hollow cop car. "Just like you, company car."

"I don't mind." I went to the passenger side of the car.

"No, no." Jack Henry rushed around his car

with his finger pointing at me to stay put. "We are going to do this the right way." He grabbed the door's handle the same time I did. "I'm going to open all of your doors tonight."

Like a good Southern woman, I let him open the door. After I got in, he ran around the car and jumped in.

"Ready?" He turned the key and started the car.

"Ready." My heart was about to jump out of my body. There were so many things that churned inside. I pulled down the hem of the short skirt, trying to cover up as much as possible, which wasn't much.

Did I bring up the clues I had found? Even though they might seem big to me, they might be insignificant to solving Ruthie's murder.

Was this a date or not? Either way, I wanted to seem like I was fun and not the funeral girl he knew.

Was he going to offer me a drink? I had never had a drop. Granny always called it truth serum. The truth was, I had been head over heels for Jack Henry Ross our entire lives. One little problem: he didn't know it and I didn't want that truth to come out.

"Okay," I waited for us to cross the county line before I got out my notebook. I had to say something. The silence was killing my nerves. "I've come up with some really solid stuff that I think you are going to be able to use to find the killer."

"Slow down." He laughed, looking over at me. He reached over. His fingers were cool and smooth as he touched my hand to put away the notebook. "We have all night to discuss what you have uncovered. Ruthie isn't going anywhere."

"But I thought you wanted to discuss the case."

"I want to have dinner with *you*." He glanced at me and then back at the road; there were touches of humor around his mouth and near his eyes.

"Oh." I put the notebook away and relaxed into my seat. "Where are we going?"

"I thought I'd take you to this little Italian place just outside of Lexington." He used the buttons on the steering wheel to turn the radio on. The cool sounds of Frank Sinatra flowed through the speakers.

"Lexington is forty minutes away." Not that I wasn't excited about being with Jack Henry Ross for forty minutes, dinner, and another forty minutes.

"Do I need to get permission from your mom and dad?" He gave a saucy wink that sent butterflies all over my body. His eyes scanned my bare legs before he looked back at the road.

"You don't have to make this out to be a date." I blew off his flirty comments. I was used to hearing all about Jack Henry's come-ons and wished it upon myself a few times, but we were adults now, not teenagers playing spin the bottle. "You and I both know that we are here to solve a crime for different reasons. You want to find a killer by using Ruthie and I want to save Granny."

"I don't think that's true." His jawline tensed visibly. "If all I wanted was information, I would have brought you in for questioning, not ask you out to dinner."

"So this is a . . ." I pointed between the two of us.

"Date?"

"Yeah, that."

"I'd like to think so." He turned his smile up a notch. "And I like your new hairstyle."

Suddenly I was blissfully happy and completely forgot about Ruthie . . . until.

"I told you that you needed a new 'do and to unbutton that blouse." Ruthie propped her kitty slippers on the middle console from the backseat. "And he doesn't want to talk about my killer, which means this is a date."

I glanced back, trying not to be so obvious, and gave her the stink eye.

"Tell Ruthie hello." He smirked, his eyes forward and his hands on the wheel. "Can't you tell her that you don't need a chaperone tonight?"

Ruthie didn't need to be told. When I looked back, she was gone. I turned around and relaxed back against the seat in relief.

"She must've heard you." I reached over and turned up the radio as Frank belted out "Fly Me to the Moon," because that was exactly how I felt.

Chapter 19

The windy country two-lane road to Lexington had always been a favorite drive with all the beautiful Kentucky bluegrass and never-ending horse farms. I had been on this road many times with Granny. She used to take us shopping in the big city before the start of school.

Charlotte always picked out the tighter shirts, shortest shorts, while I picked out the capri pants and sweaters. Not today: I glanced down at my unbuttoned blouse, resisting the urge to button a couple of them.

He did say this was a date. At the risk of looking like a sixteen-year-old love-struck teenage girl, I glanced out the window to hide my giddy smile.

Out of the corner of my eye I could tell Jack

Henry was staring at me. I shifted. I tugged at the edge of my shirt so the unbuttoned buttons lined up with the empty button holes, becoming a little more taut.

I looked over and his eyes darted up to mine.

Ahem, he cleared his throat and looked away.

"You do look nice tonight," he confirmed for the second time since I had been in the car.

By nice, I knew he meant the sexiness.

"Oh this." I blew off the fact that I had been stressed for the better part of the day about what I was going to wear.

"I don't think I've ever seen you in anything other than your capris and T-shirt or a skirt suit."

"I'm not sure wearing red-hot heels and an unbuttoned shirt would be appropriate for picking up dead bodies from their homes, or greeting mourners at the funeral home," I joked and slowly crossed my legs, letting the red high heel dangle from my toes, fully aware his eyes were taking it all in.

I tossed my hair and leaned back, looking over at him. His face reddened.

"I guess you're right." He gripped the wheel. "It's a shame I haven't seen you outside your business role. But hopefully that will change."

I turned my head toward the passenger window to cover up the smile that I couldn't force off my face. I had been dreaming about this day for many, many years and my chance was finally coming true.

The lush oak trees branched out over the road like a canopy. Jack Henry was very cautious around every turn, so I laid back and enjoyed watching all of spring's new foals gallop in all the fields.

Jack Henry turned the car onto a little side street on the outskirts of Lexington.

A small red-and-green sign that read *Bella Vino Restaurante* pointed us to a parking lot with only five parking spaces. The small red building was nestled in a wooded area. BELLA VINO was printed in white and outlined in green above the large windows that spanned the front of the restaurant. I could see inside that each front table, with large steaming family-style bowls of pasta and baskets of bread, was filled with customers.

"Are you hungry?" Jack Henry turned the car off. He put his hands in his lap and looked at me.

"Yes." I lied. I had always hated when I would hear a girl say she didn't eat much on a date because she didn't want to seem like a pig—now, I was one of those girls. It wasn't the pig part that was the issue, it was my flip-flopping stomach.

"I'm starving." He opened the door and got out. Within a second, he was opening the passenger door and holding his hand out.

After swiveling my legs, I took his hand for him to help. A brief shiver rippled through me, making me wonder if I was going to make it through the night. The place looked awfully romantic and I didn't know how to do romantic.

His hand slipped up my arm and took me by the elbow, guiding me into the restaurant.

Authentic Italian music quietly played throughout the small restaurant. There were six tables with only one open. Exposed pale-yellow-painted brick walls made it feel as though we were in Italy. Even though I'd never been to Italy, it was exactly like I would have pictured it.

Each table was covered with a cream linen tablecloth. A single candle sat in the middle for light.

Fancy. I raised an eyebrow when I looked around. I corrected my posture and clasped my hands in front of me. The tables were set with beautiful china, a napkin folded neatly on each plate, and several utensils that I had no idea what they were used for.

"Reservation for Ross." Jack Henry spoke with a smooth command when the hostess asked if she could help us.

"Right this way, please." The young woman showed us to the empty table, where the dark wooden chairs sat side by side and not across from each other. She pulled out a chair and gestured for me to sit down.

"I'd like to move my chair across the table." I pointed to the empty space between the table and the wall. The hostess picked up the chair without asking any questions.

Jack Henry blushed.

"Thank you." I smiled and sat in the chair that was now across from Jack Henry, who was gracious enough not to make any offhand comments.

The black-and-white canvas pictures that hung on the restaurant walls reminded me of the picture that had suddenly appeared at the inn after Granny had stored it in the attic. Not that they were the same. They weren't. The photos that hung on the walls were of beautiful countryside scenes that looked to me like Italy, while Ruthie's photo was just plain scary, but they were all old-looking, making them jog my memory.

"Ruthie was trying to find a next of kin." I scanned the room and noticed every couple in the place was holding hands. I folded mine in my lap.

"Two Vino Specials." Jack Henry politely smiled

at the server who was still standing next to our table.

"Thank you." She wrote down the order on her pad. "That will be right out."

After she was a good three feet away, Jack Henry leaned over with his forearms planted on the table.

"Emma Lee," he whispered, his eyes scanning the room. "The first rule in undercover work is that you can't be openly discussing what you have found out."

"Oh." I didn't even think about rules of undercover work. Nervously, I glanced around the room to see if I caught anyone staring at us. There wasn't.

Each couple was too wrapped up in their own conversations to even notice us.

"Not that they did or have been listening to us, but you always have to be ears and nose to the ground." He tapped his ear, and then his nose.

"Do you really think someone has clued in that I'm helping you?" I asked. I hadn't said a word to anyone. Had he?

"I'm not saying they are, but you never know." He stopped talking when the server came back over with an hourglass wine decanter with a ball cork stopper on top.

"Two Vino Specials are Bella's own house wine

from one of her vineyards in Italy. Would you like to try before I pour?" The server uncorked the decanter.

"No, we are fine." Jack Henry gave her the go-ahead.

She elegantly poured the two wineglasses one-quarter full before replacing the ball on the decanter and going to another table. I had the urge to put my hands out and politely turn down the wine, but I chickened out.

What was one glass going to hurt? I picked it up and smelled it, like I had seen in so many romantic movies.

"Cheers." He held his glass in the air. His eyes softly narrowed on me, making my stomach flip-flop.

I followed his lead.

"Cheers." Resisting the urge to down the whole thing, I took a drink and sat it back on the table.

Yuck! I wanted to spit what was left in my mouth back in the glass. Making sure I didn't squirm when it went down, I grabbed the chair arm and swallowed.

My question—whether or not he had mentioned to anyone that I was helping him in Ruthie's death because I could see her—burned in my gut just as much as the wine burned going down my throat.

"Have you told anyone about my . . ." I looked around like a good detective before speaking, to make sure no one was listening. I leaned over the table and whispered " . . . gift?"

I followed his eye straight to my cleavage popping out, then sat back, leaning into my chair. His eyes moved up to meet mine.

A wave of red crept up his face.

"Umm . . ." He grabbed his wineglass and took a gulp, then tugged at his collar. "No," he said hastily. "No one. I'm not sure that anyone would believe that you do see Ruthie's ghost."

"Good." I smiled, letting him off the hook for checking me out. Although I kind of liked the idea that he might be attracted to me.

Regardless, I wasn't sure if seeing Ruthie's ghost was a one-time fluke, but I sure hoped it was.

"I was going to let us enjoy the night and get to know each other better since we *really* don't know each other." He slid his hands across the table and gently laid them overtop of mine.

My chest tightened, my breath quickened. My hands slipped out from under his and I cupped my wineglass. I took another drink of wine to try to dislodge the lump in my throat. The dizzy feeling I had felt years ago when he first touched me swept over me.

How could he say we didn't really know each other? Did he forget all about the spin the bottle incident that left me scarred?

"I mean, I know we went to school together and exchange pleasantries when we pass on the street, but I don't really know what your likes and dislikes are." He took the ball off the decanter. "Would you like some more?"

I grabbed the glass and downed the wine, which I didn't like.

"Thank you." I took an even bigger sip after he filled it. "I think we know more about each other than we realize. We are from a small town."

Did he forget all the gossip? Or was he just not privy to it because he was a guy?

"I find it interesting that you see Ruthie." He tapped the glass stem. "Who else have you seen?"

"No one." I didn't want seeing ghosts to seem any crazier than it already was. I wasn't about to tell him that I saw Chicken Teater's ghost right after I was attacked by the plastic Santa. I hadn't seen Chicken Teater since, so I figured he was a fluke. Plus he'd been six feet under for many years. "Just Ruthie. Why do you ask?"

"Do you ever watch reality TV?"

"Not really." I didn't want to tell him that Charlotte was too cheap to get anything but antenna

TV in Eternal Slumber, not that there weren't reality shows on regular channels, but from what I'd heard, all the good ones were on cable.

"There's this gal in downtown Lexington and she connects people with their loved ones who have passed over." He shrugged. "It's kind of cool, that's all."

"I'm not a medium." I bit my lip. At least I didn't think I was a medium.

"Maybe you should go see someone that is and let them help you figure out the extent of your abilities." He took the napkin off the table and placed it in his lap. I followed suit. "You obviously have something if you can see and talk to Ruthie."

"I'm hoping this is a one-time gig." I smoothed the napkin in my lap. It made me nervous to think I could possibly see more ghosts. "Besides, if I could see ghosts, I'd imagine I'd see more than just Ruthie."

He smiled. Curiosity set deep in his eyes.

The server put a wood plate filled with cheeses and crackers between us.

"Your meal will be here soon." She mixed two separate sauces together in a small bowl. "Is there anything else I can get you?"

"Another vino please." He handed her the

nearly empty decanter. She poured what was left into my glass. She nodded and left.

Jack Henry picked his glass up and drank the wine like it was water. I continued to follow his lead. My taste buds were getting used to the taste.

I watched Jack Henry put a couple pieces of cheese on a cracker and spoon a little bit of the mixture, the waitress had made on top.

"They have the best cheese." He extended his little concoction to me. "You have to put on two slices to get the full sharpness."

I couldn't resist another glance at him. There was a glint of wonder in his eyes. At the same time, we both smiled.

I took a nibble off the corner of the cracker and the damn thing crumbled into my lap.

"Shit," I mumbled and swept the mess on the floor. My eyes squeezed shut just as a big sigh left my body. "Shit," I said again, with the realization that I had just brushed the mess onto the floor of the most expensive restaurant I had ever been to.

If he did notice, he was gracious enough not to mention it.

"You have to pop the entire cracker in your mouth to get the full experience." He held another cracker out to me.

I took it and followed his instructions.

"Mm." He was right. It was the best cheese cracker I had ever had or maybe it was the best date I had ever had . . . though I had to keep reminding myself that it really was a date as much as a working date. I took another drink to clear my pallet. "You know, the medium thing."

I'm not sure if it was the company, ambiance or both, but it was the best cheese I had ever tasted. And the wine . . . I didn't even like wine, but tonight it was becoming delicious.

Jack Henry was quick to fill up our glasses when the server came back. She put a family-style plate filled with different pastas between us and two empty plates.

"Then our next date in Lexington should be a date with the medium and dinner." His mouth curved with tenderness; my flesh prickled.

I wasn't sure what the Vino Special was, but it looked delicious. Having Jack Henry order without asking me made him even sexier than he already was.

Get a grip. I downed the wine and helped myself to some more. I had to think about something else and thinking about Ruthie was a sure way of killing the strong attraction I was having toward Jack Henry.

"Did you hear what I said about the next of kin for Ruthie?" It was a big piece of information that seemed to hold some answers.

"The next of kin does have me interested." He twirled the spaghetti noodles on his plate.

He even looked hot eating noodles. I forced myself to look away and down at my plate of pasta. I didn't bother with the noodles, I went straight for the cheese-filled ravioli.

"You know Granny is redecorating the place and she put all of Ruthie's things in the attic." The wine went well with the pasta. I took another drink. "I'm sure it is because she wants the developer to give her top dollar for the inn. But that is beside the point."

I briefly told him about the ugly picture, including the details of the people and how it was brought back downstairs by someone other than Granny.

"Ruthie made sure I took it home." I gladly accepted another glass of wine when Jack Henry gestured. "That was what I was getting out of the hearse when you pulled up."

"You had some sort of box too."

"I haven't opened it." I filled my plate with more food. "I haven't had time. I'm not even sure what it is. Ruthie didn't even say anything about it. I'm sure it's not hers."

"The mayor told me the meeting got really heated between Zula and that girl that works there." He sat back and wiped his mouth.

"Hettie Bell." I pointed my fork at him before I stabbed another ravioli and put it in my mouth. "She's a weirdo."

With a mouthful, I was still able to tell him about the meeting and how I had seen Hettie at Girl's Best Friend Spa.

"She did have motive to be mad at Ruthie, but I'm not sure if she had enough anger to kill her."

"What did she do?" He rested his elbows on the table.

"She asked for a day off. Ruthie told her no, but Granny let her take it." My body seemed to have melted back into the chair.

Everything around me started to slow down. My heart. My breathing. The people around me. Even Jack Henry's lips moved in slow motion. I watched in a strange inner emotion of excitement thinking about his lips on mine.

"That could go against Zula too." He waved his fork in front of me. "Emma Lee, are you okay?"

"Better than okay." I bit my lip seductively. "Ouch." I pressed my lips together after I bit it a little too seductively.

His brows furrowed. "I said that Zula letting Hettie off for the day could also work against her."

"But there is something about Hettie that I can't put my finger on." I tapped the wineglass, and then looked up.

Jack Henry suddenly became the most handsome guy I had ever seen, including any movie star out there.

"What?" His infectious grin set the tone.

"You are one good . . ." I stopped myself before I made more of a mockery of myself and professed my attraction to him. I pushed the glass away from me. "You are good at making me drink more wine than I should."

He reached across the table for my hand.

"I think you've had enough to drink." He patted me.

"No." I laughed him off. "I'm fine."

I lied, but was good at keeping it together. Or so I thought.

"What do you think about my clues so far?" Maybe my quick skills of crime-solving were a turn-on to him. Plus I was curious to know if I was on the right track.

"You've got some good stuff here." He waved his hand in the air to signal the server that we were ready for the check. "Now that the mayor is going to run for governor, she's on my ass about solving this murder."

"Oh, yeah." I rolled my eyes remembering how she acted when she came into Girl's Best Friend Spa. "She was on the phone with someone in Frankfort when she came into the salon to get her hair done."

"She is dead set on becoming governor. And I wouldn't put it past her to win either." He took out his wallet and laid some twenties in the black tray the server had left. "You ready?"

"I am." Sadness filled me when I realized the night was almost over.

Sure, he reached over and touched my hand, glanced at my legs, but not once had he tried to kiss me.

The room spun around when I stood up. I steadied myself and blamed it on my heels.

After he helped me back in the car, I planted my face on the window. The cold felt so good. I propelled my back to the seat when Jack Henry got in because I didn't want him to know or figure out that he was right . . . I had had too much to drink.

The first glass was too many, considering that I never drink.

"Are you ready for that karaoke?" He put the car in gear.

"You aren't serious, are you?" In a moment of crazy, I reached over and put my hand on his leg, giving it a little squeeze.

Immediately he looked down and then over at me. His lip curled up. "Yes, Emma Lee, I'm kidding."

I let out a big sigh and leaned over, kissing him on the cheek. "Thank you." I floated back to my side and leaned my head back on the headrest, relieved he wasn't going to follow through with embarrassing me.

"I think it's best to get you home."

I waved my hand in the air. Suddenly I was too tired to even open my eyes.

Before I knew it, we were back in Sleepy Hollow and he was helping me out of the car.

I wasn't sure if it was the full moon or just Jack Henry in general, but he looked so good.

"Do you remember the time we played spin the bottle?" I stumbled and he wrapped his big strong arms around me, standing me up against the car. "You," I jabbed his chest, "you got up and ran off when the bottle stopped on me and not Miss Hot Pants." I snapped my fingers in the air. "What was her name?"

"I don't know." He shook his head and laughed. For some reason, he found me to be amusing.

"Well, you hurt my feelings," I slurred and wiped my mouth with the backside of my hand. "Was it 'cause you didn't want to kiss the scary funeral girl?"

"No, Emma Lee." The moon cast down on his face. His jaw clenched. And his five-o'clock shadow begged to be rubbed.

I lifted my hand to his face and stroked the whiskers. He pulled away.

"Emma Lee, I think we better get you inside." He put my arm around his shoulder and his arm held me up around my waist. Suddenly my legs wouldn't work. He hoisted me in his arms, cradling me like a baby.

"I declare," a gasp came from behind us. "It's only eight o'clock at night. What a shame."

I whipped my head back over Jack Henry's shoulder to find Beulah Paige Bellefry on the sidewalk with her hands planted on her hips, taking in the entire scene.

"Good evening, Ms. Bellefry." Jack Henry didn't pay her any attention and continued to walk with me draped in his arms like he would his dry cleaning.

"Yeah, go on and tell your hoity-toity friends about this!" I yelled over his shoulder and pointed at her. "We have a history together!" I pointed from me to Jack Henry. "We played spin the bottle! Go tell them that, you busybody!" I put my hand on his shoulder and squeezed. "You sure have some strong shoulders," I murmured.

"Emma Lee." He hugged me closer.

"What?" I kept my eyes closed and rested my head on his shoulder. "She is evil. And if she tries to spread gossip about us, I will get her."

"No you won't."

Faintly I remember Jack saying something about water after he put me in bed, but as soon as he covered me with Granny's quilt, I was out.

Chapter 20

'm coming!" I held my head in my hands and peeled myself out of bed when I heard someone trying to beat down my private-residence door at Eternal Slumber.

Bang, bang, bang!

"I'm coming!" I screamed and glanced in the dresser mirror on the way out of my bedroom. "Oh my gosh."

I tried to rack my fingers through my new layered hairstyle that could no longer be classified as a style. The shorter layers were sticking up on the sides while the back was flat to my head. I wiped my fingers underneath my eyes to get off the smeared mascara.

Groaning, I rubbed my temples. My head was killing me.

Bang, bang, bang!

Without even looking at who was making all this commotion, I whipped the door open.

"Jack Henry?" I smacked my head when I remembered how I had gotten home last night. I rubbed my head and held the door open. "Ouch. Come on in."

He was back in his Sleepy Hollow uniform, hat placed strategically on top. He stepped in, his eyes gazing downward.

I looked down to see what he was looking at.

"Oh gosh." I fumbled to button up the blouse I had on from last night. In fact, I was wearing all of the same clothes from last night, even the red high heels.

"I'm so sorry about last night." I tried to smile, but it hurt every single bone in my body to even think about it. I flung each of my feet, sending the high heels in different directions. Jack Henry ducked. "No coffee?"

I tried to make a joke, but quickly noticed that Jack was in no joking mood.

"Ah, oh." Ruthie eyed him. "What happened last night?"

I ignored her, running my fingers along my hair and then wrapping my arms around my waist.

"He doesn't look happy to see you." She shot her glance in my direction. "What did you do last night? He was yours—hook, line and sinker. But now it looks like you made a stinker." She snickered. I didn't find it too amusing.

I had completely screwed up any opportunity to ever go on a real date with him, much less have a dating future. He wasn't even being the Southern gentleman that I knew by taking off his hat.

"I'm sorry." I started to apologize. "I *rarely* drink. Maybe one cocktail a week and I should have told you that little fact about me before I drank all of that wine last night."

"We have a problem." He stood with his legs apart like the police officers you see on those shows. He ignored my apology. "Beulah Paige Bellefry was found strangled."

"Strangled?" I gasped, putting my hands up to my neck. Suddenly my headache got worse.

"Luckily, she isn't dead . . . yet."

"Serves her right." Ruthie tapped her kitty slipper. "She puts her nose in everyone's business. Anyone could've tried to kill her."

Hello pot . . . was what I wanted to say to Ruthie,

but kept my mouth shut. Jack wasn't happy and it was no time to be fooling around with a ghost.

"Yet?" My eyes widened and I ignored Ruthie. Jack Henry's news was getting worse by the minute.

"She's in the hospital on life support." He narrowed his gaze. "Did you leave your bed after I put you in it last night?"

"Does it look like it?" I looked down. I had the exact same outfit on that I had been left in. "Why would you say something like that anyway?"

Gosh, the last thing I remember, Jack Henry and I had a great time last night.

He pulled his little notebook out of his jacket pocket and flipped it open.

"According to some eyewitnesses, you were seen at Higher Grounds fighting with her, not to mention last night's encounter."

"Last night?" I bit my lip trying to remember something about Beulah. Suddenly I realized that we had seen her, but didn't recall any words. "What about last night?"

Jack Henry's gaze narrowed with a burning question deep in his eyes. "You don't remember me carrying you into the funeral home and Beulah walking down the street?"

"Oh!" I raised my hand to my mouth with a

shiver of vivid recollection. "Now, Jack. You know I would never hurt Beulah."

"People do odd things when gossip is spread around about them." He wrote something in the notebook.

I wanted to grab that little pad out of his hands and rip it to shreds, but resisted the urge. I didn't want to go to jail for assault of an officer.

"Seriously?" I planted one hand on my hip and the other on the throbbing vein that ran down my left temple.

"Let's just say that we," he gestured between us, "need to be on the down-low. But I have to tell you that I can't ignore your comments to Beulah last night."

"You'll see. When she wakes up, she'll tell you it wasn't me." Oh, how I wished she'd wake up. "She will wake up, right?"

He shook his head. "The doctors don't know. They said that she was barely hanging on when John Howard Lloyd found her."

"John Howard found her?" My wheels turned. He was going to be doing some graveyard work for Eternal Slumber today. I'm sure he'd let me in on all the details of finding Beulah and maybe a few clues could come out of it.

"He did. Around three this morning."

It wouldn't be unusual for John Howard to be roaming the streets at three A.M. I had to get Jack Henry out of there.

"If you aren't going to arrest me, then I need to go get ready for my day." There was no sense in trying to flirt with him. I was sure he was thinking that I was now a suspect, but since Beulah was still alive, he couldn't arrest me for murder.

Please, please stay alive, I secretly prayed.

"I'm not." He stepped back out of the door. "But I still can't ignore your comment. Vernon Baxter said the autopsy should be done on Ruthie soon. There may be some questions I need to ask her. You will be around, right?" He looked at me as if he was telling me not to pack my bags and run.

"We aren't Thelma and Louise." I referred to me and Ruthie, then I leaned on the door with my arms crossed.

"Fine." He flipped his notebook shut and put it back in his Velcro pocket. "Really? One cocktail a week?"

I shook my head and bit my lip.

"Huh." He walked to his car, never turning back around.

Normally, I'd watch him and his car until it was out of sight, but not today. I suddenly had a to-do list a mile long. I had to get cleaned up and ready to check things off the list. The picture in my office was first on the list, along with talking to John Howard Lloyd.

"Did you see any funny business outside last night?" I questioned Ruthie while getting ready, to see if she saw what had happened to Beulah.

I grabbed my toothbrush and put a mound of toothpaste on it. After-drinking breath was not a good smell to wake up to.

"No. I only pay attention to you because you can see me." She scowled. "I have a sneaky suspicion someone has gone from framing Zula to framing you."

"What?" I spit in the sink before I could continue to scrub my teeth.

"Think about it." Ruthie paced back and forth in the small bathroom behind me. "Originally they tried to pin it on Zula with the development of the inn, but quickly shifted when they found out you were sticking your nose into things and having public fights with Beulah."

"Huh?" Toothpaste dripped from my gaping open mouth. Who would create such an elaborate plan and why? Someone with something big at stake. Suddenly, my little headache had turned into a migraine.

"Think about it." Ruthie's bony finger tapped

her temple. "They want the heat off of them for murdering me, for God knows why. But now you look just crazy enough to have fallen off your rocker and gone on a killing spree."

"I'd hardly call this a killing spree."

"It is for Sleepy Hollow." She reminded me that we had never had crime like this before.

"*Thanks.*" My voice was low and sarcastic.

I rinsed my mouth out and grabbed a couple of pain relievers. What Ruthie said made sense. Which led me to more questions.

Now I had to find out who was behind the murder and attack, not only for Granny's sake, but for my own.

Chapter 21

"Where are you?" I phoned Charlotte when I noticed she wasn't at work. Completely out of her normal routine, which made me a nervous wreck since she was always the sensible one and always on time.

"I had to go into Lexington with the stuff Granny told me." She put my anxiety to ease.

"You talked to Granny?" I was anxious to hear what Granny's explanation was about the taxes.

"Yes. She said she did pay the taxes. She gave me a copy of the ledger and her accounting files. Earl kept a meticulous file system." There was a bit of relief in Charlotte's voice. "She said she left all the original ledgers in the storage at Eternal Slumber, but I couldn't find any of them."

"Do you have the copies?" This was probably the best news we could have gotten about the tax-evasion claims.

"I do. I'm taking them to the accountant now." Charlotte's voice stilled. "I'm scared that someone has planned this all along."

"Planned what?"

"I think someone took Granny's payments and killed Ruthie to set her up." Her voice dropped in volume. "Earl had a separate account for the taxes and the money has been taken out, but the checks that were written to the IRS were cashed and not by the IRS. Granny and I went to the bank and no one can seem to figure out where the money went or who took it out. I'm scared, Emma Lee."

"We will figure this out. Just be careful," I warned her. "They found Beulah practically strangled to death last night."

"Oh no," Charlotte gasped. "Is she . . ."

"No, she isn't dead—yet." I decided not to inform her of my little comment about getting back at Beulah if she spread a rumor about me and Jack Henry. "Jack Henry said that she was on life support."

"Emma Lee." Charlotte's voice escalated. "I completely forgot. How was your date? Granny couldn't stop talking about how happy she was that you were going out with Jack Henry."

"It was good." I didn't really lie this time. It was good, up until I had too much wine. "We had a nice dinner at that little Italian place on the outskirts of Lexington."

"Bella Vino?"

"Yeah, how do you know the place?"

"Emma Lee, I don't spend all my time with the dead." She laughed. "Listen, I'm here. I'll let you know what I find out."

Without letting me say good-bye or be careful, Charlotte hung up.

I crossed off the tax-evasion thing on my figure-things-out to-do-list, and was happy that Charlotte had spoken to Granny about it and there was some sort of trail. But where did it go wrong? Who could possibly have stolen Granny's money? Could it be tied to Ruthie's murder? And if it was tied to Ruthie's murder, had this person planned it out for years?

"There you are." I was happy to see Ruthie in my office. The closet door was shut, but Ruthie stood outside it.

"I've been looking at this picture." She pointed, but I couldn't see what she was pointing to.

"Move out of the way." Having to put my hand through Ruthie's ghost to open the closet door wasn't on my list. The thought gave me the heebie-jeebies.

The picture was leaning up against the closet wall with the tin box next to it. I took both of them out to get a good look.

The picture was old. The paper backing it was mounted on had rips in two corners.

"You think there is some tie-in to your history here?" I questioned Ruthie.

"Yes," she said softly.

"Are you going to get upset if I tear this backing off?"

She shook her head.

There was no saving the paper when I peeled it off. It was dry-rotted and crumbled into pieces without my help.

I brushed my hand over the back of the picture to get off the dust. There was some writing in the corner. I got closer to read it.

"Slicklizzard, Kentucky?" Now, there were some strange counties in Kentucky, but I'd never heard of Slicklizzard.

"Oh!" The eyes on Ruthie's kitty cat slippers jingled as she bounced up and down. "Earl Way mentioned Slicklizzard a few times."

Ruthie bent down and looked at the name. She stood back up. Her mouth and eyes turned down.

"What's wrong?" I asked. "We have a name to start with. I can go to Slick . . ." I looked at the name again, " . . . Slicklizzard and do some research at the courthouse in the records room."

She shook her head. Tears filled her eyes.

"I can find your next of kin," I assured her.

"I think this is Earl's family, not mine." She touched the picture. "He had fond memories of being in Slicklizzard as a boy."

"Still?" I shrugged. "You said it spoke to you."

"It's probably because it was Earl's."

I turned around to look at her, but she was gone.

Without hesitation, I opened the old tin box. There were a couple of pictures, some old coins and a tarnished ring.

It was a man's ring with an old family coat of arms, with a shield as the focal point and the name Payne engraved in a banner at the top. Triangular red rubies garnished the two top points of the shield. There was a triangular hole at the bottom point of the shield; I came to the conclusion that it was missing a ruby.

This was obviously Earl's. He had probably put

it up in the attic since it didn't have much value.

I put the ring back in the tin box and took out one of the old photos, an old snapshot, in particular, that had caught my eye. The edges had yellowed from aging.

It was the exact same picture as the big framed one from Slicklizzard. I flipped it over.

"Slicklizzard, Kentucky," I read out loud. "Earl Way Payne, Becky Dawn Payne, Dugger Bob Payne." A few more names were listed.

I flipped the picture back and forth. Someone had taken the time to write the names of all the individuals on the back. Something Granny would've done with her pictures so we would have known what family was who when she was dead and gone to the great beyond.

I snickered looking at Earl Way. He looked to be a rascal as a boy. Thank God he'd had his teeth fixed. I couldn't help but zero in on his crooked smile.

Ruthie Sue was right. This old stuff was probably nothing. It was Earl's junk. Nothing more, nothing less. There were a few other odd things in the box, but nothing significant to help solve Ruthie's murder.

I was still going to tell Granny about the stuff.

She'd get a kick out of it. But then again, she'd probably already seen it.

I stuck the picture and box back in the closet and shut the door. I was back to square one. There was no time to wallow in self-pity. There was still a murder to solve, not to mention the assault on Beulah.

The next clue that would help clear Granny was the fact that she had a solid alibi the night Ruthie was murdered—Doc Clyde.

I reached into my bag and pulled out Zula Fae Raines Payne's file. If Granny ever decided to get remarried, they'd have to extend her file tab somehow.

There were a lot of regular things in there that Granny had seen Doc Clyde for, but nothing that looked to be alarming.

"Last visit." I paged through the file and reached the end. I dragged my finger down the page to the last entry. "March 2012?"

I read it again. "March 2012? Over a year ago?"

But her eye didn't twitch. I recalled her reaction when I asked her about her alibi when Ruthie and I paid her a visit after Jack Henry had told me about his suspicions that Ruthie was murdered.

Granny was up to something. The taxes . . . the

lying about going to the doctor . . . in the back of my head, I knew Doc Clyde wasn't open at three A.M., but I knew someone that was. Well, not open, but up. Cheryl Lynne Doyle and John Howard Lloyd.

Chapter 22

It wasn't long after I wrote Cheryl Lynn Doyle and John Howard's names in my sleuth notebook that I heard John Howard's heavy footsteps coming up the front steps of Eternal Slumber, through the hall and down the stairs to the basement, where the morgue, tools and prepping rooms were located.

He was a sucker for a hot cup of coffee—my ticket to get him to talk.

"Morning, John Howard." I held out a cup of coffee that I had poured before I came down to ask him my questions. The coffee would help break the ice before I started to drill him with questions about Beulah and the night of Ruthie's murder. "I brought you down a cup of coffee."

He reached out his dirt-stained hand and took

the cup. "Thank you, Miss Emma." He smiled. The steam from the coffee curled around his nose when he held it up to his mouth. "That's good coffee."

"Why, thank you." I looked around. He was cleaning the tools that he needed for digging graves.

"Are you sure you don't want a machine to help?" I asked, hoping new equipment would change his mind about leaving.

With the new equipment out there, I had offered to buy John Howard something different than the little backhoe he liked to use along with a few shovels, but he always refused.

"No, ma'am." He flexed his arms. "I like the workout it gives me. But the rate we are going with deaths, I might not be able to keep up with the work."

What work? In case John Howard had been under a rock lately, no one was using Eternal Slumber for their beloved ones' final resting stop.

"You mean with Ruthie and now the attack on Beulah?" I couldn't have planned his timing any better.

I walked around the room and pretended to take inventory so he wouldn't think I was being nosy.

"It's a shame." He shook his head and took another drink. "Someone is preying on the elderly women in the community."

"I would hardly call Beulah old at forty-two." I referred to Beulah's age.

"She's only forty-two?" He pulled back in shock. "She hangs out with the older Auxiliary women; I thought she was older than that."

"You are out pretty late, aren't you?"

"I guess you could say that." He sat his cup on the old metal shelf and used a worn rag and paint thinner to clean the blade of one of the shovels. "I don't sleep much, so I walk around."

"That's what I wanted to talk to you about." I picked up another one of his rags and dipped it in the tin of paint thinner. I grabbed the shovel and cleaned the dirt from the blade. "These attacks are happening in the middle of the night. You and I both know that Granny didn't kill Ruthie, but I have a sneaky suspicion she is a suspect."

John Howard put the rag and tool down. His eyes narrowed, casting a shadow on his face. No one messed with Granny when John Howard was around. After all, she was the only one in town who had given him a chance and a job when he came to town.

"And I wanted to know if you saw anything or anyone out of the ordinary that might give me a lead on who to ask if they saw anything."

"You know"—his eyes lit up as if he remembered something—"on two occasions I saw someone that I know doesn't live here walking around three A.M. I know it was the same person because they had on overalls and some crazy hair. I'm sure it was one of them hippie visitors going camping or hiking the caves."

"Do you remember the days?" I was getting somewhere, I knew it, though it wouldn't be unusual for hikers to come into town. But in the middle of the night?

"Yea," He scratched his head. "One was the night before I heard Ruthie died and the other was last night."

"Are you sure?"

"Positive." He nodded. "Especially last night. How was your date with Jack Henry?"

"I'm guessing you saw that?" I questioned in an apologetic tone.

"Not your finest hour." His mouth turned up in a crooked grin. "If Beulah wasn't in the hospital, I'd probably be laughing right now."

"Yeah, me too, John Howard. Me too." I picked up my mug and went back upstairs.

There was at least one person of interest sneaking around Sleepy Hollow, and I had a description.

Before I forgot what John Howard told me, I wrote it in my notebook.

I grabbed my purse, locked the door to Eternal Slumber and headed straight for Higher Grounds Café.

Hettie Bell crossed the street from the square and into the courthouse. She had papers in her hand, which made me wonder if she got all those signatures she needed in order to stop the development.

Cheryl Lynne wasn't going anywhere and I was curious to see what Hettie was up to. I snuck up the courthouse steps and slipped in the door.

Hettie went into a room with a sign hanging over the door that read RECORDS.

"Morning, Emma Lee." Mayor May sashayed down the hall, sporting an all-white one-piece dress and electric-blue high heels. "What are you doing in here this morning?"

"I was . . ." I bit my lip. I had to think fast. "I wanted to talk to you."

"Well, you are in luck." Her eyebrows rose and so did her lips. "I have about five minutes before my meeting with my new campaign manager." She took me by the arm and guided me toward her office—the opposite direction of Hettie. "Isn't this exciting!" She let go and put her hands up in the air like she was framing something. "Small-town mayor becomes the governor." She sighed with happiness.

"Yeah, great." I smiled.

Being mayor must be pretty nice. Her office was as big as Eternal Slumber. The biggest oriental rug I had ever seen lay on top of the hardwood floor. There was a floor-to-ceiling wooden bookshelf that spanned the entire length of her office, filled with books.

"I've read them all," she said when she noticed I was staring at them. "Reading is knowledge, Emma Lee. Knowledge is power. You remember that."

Her desk sat in front of the bookshelf wall. Her view was phenomenal with the tall windows overlooking the square.

"I see it all." She walked over to the windows, folded her arms across her body and looked out. "What did you want, Emma Lee?"

She turned on her heels, with her arms still crossed.

"I wanted to ask you about this development thing." I lied, but it would be good to know. "Hettie Bell is determined to stop it and I think it might be good for the community."

"You do?"

"Charlotte is always telling me that we need to support the community more and this might be a good way to do it."

"Does she?"

"Yes, ma'am." I was beginning to think the mayor knew I wasn't at the courthouse to see her.

"I'll keep that in mind when the town votes and if Hettie gets the signatures, but for now, Zula and I are in talks with the development company." She slinked back to her desk and sat in the large leather chair. "We will provide an update in the *Journal*. Thank you for your time."

It was my cue to leave.

"Thank you for listening to me." I gave a slight wave to leave.

"Emma Lee," she called after me. I turned around. "I like your new haircut."

I brushed my hands through the layered tresses. "Thanks."

Just as I walked out of the office, Hettie was walking to the exit. I rushed into the records room, where the deputy county clerk was putting away some files.

"I'll be with you in a minute." She stood on a stool and pushed in a record book.

I watched and counted over to the ledger she

was replacing. I had to know what Hettie had requested. The record had to be what Hettie had asked to see, because they didn't let you retrieve your own material. That was the job of the deputy clerk.

"Now." She brushed her hands together. "Getting those P's kills me every time." She smiled. "What can I help you with?"

"I need to see any records on . . ." *P? Payne?* "Payne."

"You are the third person who has come in here researching the Paynes." She sighed.

"My granny is a Payne and I'm working on a family tree." *Why would Hettie be looking up Payne?* "Is there any way I can request the records be copied?"

"Sure, but it's going to be a day or so." She brushed her bangs out of her eyes. "I'm swamped."

"Sure." I really didn't care about records here. I had to make a trip to Slicklizzard, Kentucky. Hettie was trying to dig up some dirt and I had to know all I could.

Who was Hettie Bell? Where did she come from? And why was she so interested in the Paynes or saving the Sleepy Hollow Inn?

Chapter 23

After I left the courthouse, I went back to my office and marked John Howard's name off the list of people to see.

"Cheryl Lynne Doyle." I tapped her name and pictured her with long blond hair and perfect body as she happily made those delicious doughnuts. Looks, brains and talent . . . *ugh*. "I'm coming to see you, Cheryl Lynne."

I threw my notebook in my purse and flung it over my shoulder.

Within minutes I had the hearse pulled into a parking space right in front of Higher Grounds Café.

"I think Earl has a past." Ruthie came out of nowhere, slipping up to me when I walked up on the sidewalk. "The more I think about the items you found and things he'd say, something is not adding up."

"I understand that, but he is dead." I rushed around the corner of Higher Grounds so I could talk to her without someone seeing me and accusing me of the "Funeral Trauma." On second thought . . . "Earl didn't kill you, Ruthie Sue Payne!"

If I was getting set up for murder and now an attack, I wanted people seeing me act crazy so I could claim insanity, just in case.

A few people turned to watch me have my conversation with Ruthie's ghost, only they just saw me talking to the air.

"He is dead. How can a dead person kill you?" I questioned the air around me and twirled.

"What are you doing?" Ruthie whispered as if someone could hear her. She tugged at my sleeve for me to shut up. "They are going to lock you up. You said so yourself."

"Good morning!" I yelled at a couple of the Auxiliary women standing outside of the café with their hands across their mouths as they stared at the crazy girl . . . me, before I headed on in.

"I've been to see Beulah." Ruthie stopped right in front of me. I closed my eyes and walked right through her. A surge of electricity sent a jolt through me. "Are you listening to me?"

I gave a slight nod for her to continue.

"She has the same pinch on her neck that I have on my back."

Okay, that stopped me dead in my tracks.

"Hi, Emma Lee." Cheryl Lynne was wiping off the countertop. "Zula nearly bought me out of doughnuts this morning."

"I'll be right back." I did a pee-pee dance, pretending I needed to use the restroom. I shut the bathroom door behind me and locked it. "Spill."

"I obviously know you didn't try to kill Beulah, so I went to the hospital." She paced the small room back and forth. "She isn't dead, but close to it."

"Get back to the pinch mark," I coaxed her to hurry up. I didn't want Cheryl to think I *was* crazy.

"They tried to use their hands, but I heard Jack Henry talking to the doctors." She wrung her hands. "They said that someone had cleaned off their prints because they thought she was dead, but she had a faint pulse that couldn't be detected by touch, only machine. I got real close to look and see if they had big hands or small hands, just like you asked me, and there it was."

"What?" I waited with baited breath.

"A mark just like mine on the right side of her neck."

"Right side? Yours was on the left." I reminded her.

"I didn't see my attacker, but I bet Beulah did!" Ruthie snapped her fingers in the air, before she pretended to strangle the air.

I followed suit and put my hands in the air like I had someone around the neck and then I put them down like I was pushing someone.

"I think you have something." I smiled and pulled my notebook out of my purse and jotted down what Ruthie had seen. "Did Jack Henry say anything about it?"

"No, not a word and neither did the doctors." Slowly she shook her head. "Now I know someone is trying to set you up."

Her words made me shiver, sending goose bumps up my legs and arms.

"What do you mean? The police know I didn't kill you." I was confused.

"No, but now the killer knows that you are investigating this and now they have tried to pin Beulah on you." She looked up. Terror lay deep in her eyes, her brows furrowed with worry. "Someone is out to get you and Zula."

Knock, knock, knock.

I jumped when someone knocked on the door, bringing me back to the living.

"Washing my hands," I hollered and grabbed a paper towel before opening the door.

"Emma Lee!" Mary Anna's red lips curved up. "Oh . . ." She took me by the arm and led me back into the bathroom. She locked the door behind her and threw herself up against it. "Spill it!"

"Spill what?" For a brief second I freaked out. My palms sweating, I grabbed another paper towel and wiped them. Did she know I was trying to figure out who killed Ruthie? Did she know I could see Ruthie?

"Your date with Jack Henry." She bounced in her white short dress that resembled the iconic dress Marilyn Monroe wore in *The Seven Year Itch*. "You know what Marilyn said."

"No, what?" I had no idea of anything Marilyn said unless it came out of Mary Anna's mouth.

"Sex is part of nature, and I go along with nature." She grinned. "So . . . tell me."

"There is nothing to tell." I pretended to lock my lips with my fingers.

"No one can go on a date with that hunk and say nothing to tell." She batted her heavily laden eyelashes, exposing the silvery glittered eye shadow. "You aren't one of those girls who doesn't give details, are you?"

"I guess I am." I shrugged and pushed past her, letting myself out of the bathroom.

"I expect details when you come in for a trim-up in a couple weeks," she hollered after me. "I'll put you on the books and tell you the appointment when I see you at Eternal Slumber."

"You do that," I said over my shoulder. I was definitely going to keep up the hair appointments, but nothing was going to get these lips to talk.

Everyone knows that loose lips sink ships, and I was already doing a good job of that without the help of gossip.

"Can I get a cup of coffee?" I sat down at the counter.

"Coming up." Cheryl grabbed a mug and filled it up. She sat it in front of me and leaned on the glass top. Her hair tumbled over her shoulder. "Thanks for talking to Zula about the doughnuts."

"Sure. Can I ask you a question?" I glanced around the café. No one was staring at us. The coast was clear. "You know that Granny is an obvious suspect in Ruthie's death and I'm trying to figure out how to prove she didn't do it."

"Yeah."

"You mentioned that you get up and bake doughnuts at three A.M." I took a quick sip. "Did you happen to see anyone unusual around that time?"

"I didn't want to say anything, nor spread gossip, but now that you asked . . ." She hesitated and then waved her hand in the air. "I saw three people that night." She leaned in closer; her gaze darted around before she realized no one was watching. She lowered her voice. "I saw Zula and Doc Clyde going into his office around three A.M. and some camper over in the square."

So Granny was with Doc Clyde? But why three A.M.?

"Are you sure it was Granny?"

"Yes."

"Okay." I shook my head. That was a question for Granny. "What about the camper? Did they have on overalls and crazy hair?"

She nodded.

"Man or woman?"

"I couldn't tell." She pulled back. "I was so taken off guard by Zula and Clyde that I didn't pay much attention to the camper."

"How do you know it was a camper?"

She shrugged. "I don't. I just assumed it was someone here for the caves."

A customer sat down in the seat next to me and looked over the menu.

"Thanks, Cheryl." I got up and waved bye. She gave a slight smile as if it had pained her to tell me about Granny's late-night visit.

Was Granny sick and not telling me, or anyone, for that matter? What about this camper?

John Howard and Cheryl Lynne both saw someone around the time of the murder, three A.M., but who was it? And why were they in Sleepy Hollow?

Chapter 24

The next item on my list was to visit Slick-lizzard, Kentucky, to investigate exactly who *was* in that picture.

From John Howard and Cheryl Lynne's descriptions, the Midnight Murderer—my new nickname for the killer, which I thought was very clever since it reminded me of the exposés on *Dateline NBC*—looked a lot like the persons in the photo. Creepy.

But I had another order of business to take care of before I headed out of town.

Talk to Charlotte.

I pulled the hearse in front of Eternal Slumber—not my normal parking space, but I was in a hurry. I had to tell Charlotte about Granny's midnight trip to Doc Clyde's and see if she could wiggle the truth out of Granny.

I dashed up the front steps and into the vestibule.

"Charlotte?" I yelled into the funeral home. If anyone knew something about Granny being sick, it was probably going to be Charlotte. "Charlotte?"

Granny had a tendency to keep life issues from me because of the "Funeral Trauma," and if she did have something seriously wrong, which I'm sure she did, because she would never call the doctor in the middle of the night, she would tell Charlotte.

I stomped into Charlotte's office, mad.

"I do not have the . . ." *Funeral Trauma* was what I was going to say, but decided to save my energy when Charlotte wasn't in her office. In fact, her office hadn't been touched since she left to go figure out Granny's tax issue. I glanced out her office window and noticed that her car wasn't there, which meant she was still in Lexington dealing with the tax-evasion scandal.

What if Granny needed to sell the inn in order to pay for her sickness? All sorts of things circled my head as I walked back to my office.

I flicked the light on and went over to sit down in the desk chair but stumbled when the lights went out.

I froze. I thought I was hearing the sound of my heavy breathing, but I wasn't.

"The lights didn't accidently go off, did they?" I gulped, lightly patting my desk for any type of sharp tool. There was a hint of light coming from the pulled drapes.

Stop, drop, and roll. My mind repeated the mantra the teachers stuck in our heads. *Only if it was a fire.* I held my breath and listened for any movement from the intruder.

I had to somehow crawl over to the window and open the curtains.

Suddenly, an arm went around my neck. I was yanked back so hard, my feet came out from under me. Evidently the intruder didn't want me to fall, but I did and I rolled onto my knees, scrambling toward the door.

My ears buzzed, but I could still hear someone reaching out into the dark feeling around for me.

"Nosy!" The voice was harsh and cold. I couldn't make out if it was male or female, but I did know that I had to get the hell out of there or I was really going to be laid out next to Ruthie.

When something grabbed my ankle, I kicked it and hit something.

"Son of . . ."

It wasn't enough for them to let go. They

dragged me by my ankle, spinning me around before they let go and flung me into the two chairs in front of my desk, which made me realize where I was in my office.

Pain racketed inside my head. I felt something warm trickle down my cheek.

"Oh my God!" I was sure I had been shot. "Help!" I screamed for anyone, anything to hear me.

If John Howard, Vernon Baxter, or Mary Anna were there, they'd be in the basement, where all the work takes place. And that was the best insulated place on earth.

I struggled up to my feet by holding on to the chair arms. Adrenaline took over and I picked the chair up, swinging it in the dark like a windmill until I made it over to the window and yanked the curtain down.

"Hold it!" Jack Henry yelled from the hall when the intruder ran out of my office.

I rushed out after the intruder, who I could see was wearing overalls and a ski mask.

"Out of the way!" Jack Henry yelled at me, the intruder stuck between us.

There was no way I was letting this person get away. I lunged toward him. He dodged, grabbing me by the arm and throwing me into Jack Henry.

It took a minute for us to untangle ourselves and Jack Henry to jump up and run out the door after whoever was there to kill me.

"Shit! Emma Lee!" Jack Henry stumbled back into the funeral home. I hadn't moved from where he left me.

"I've been shot." I held my hand on my cheek as the blood dripped to the floor.

Jack Henry rushed over and kneeled down beside me.

He moved my hand and held my face, tilting it at all angles.

"You haven't been shot." He pulled me to my feet. "You have a gash in your head that will probably require stitches."

"I'm not going to the hospital." I shook my head. If Vernon was downstairs, he'd be able to do a little stitching for me. "Did you see where he went?"

"No." He put his gun back in his holster. "Why did you go after him?"

"Because," I groaned. I went back into my office and into the bathroom. Jack Henry followed and flipped on every single light switch on the way. "I couldn't let him get away."

"Emma Lee, I told you to leave it to the police."

He took my head and tilted it toward the bathroom light. He took the hand towel and dampened it before putting it on my head.

After he sat me in my office chair, he got me a glass of water and retrieved Vernon from the basement.

As Vernon stitched me up, I briefly told them what I had learned about Granny's midnight doctor's visit and I how I was coming back to ask Charlotte if Granny was ill when I was attacked.

"Clyde and Zula have gone out on a few dates," Vernon casually said as his elbow went up and down in the air with each new stitch he was putting into my scalp.

"What?" I screeched; my head pounded.

"She didn't tell you about it?" Vernon pulled on the thread, I grimaced. "Ruthie and I went on a double date with them a week before Ruthie was murdered."

My mouth dropped. I suddenly felt faint. There was a lot about Granny I didn't know.

"They make a nice couple." Jack Henry smiled. He looked at me playfully. He knew the new information about Granny's love life was killing me.

"That means"—I jumped up and kissed Vernon on the cheek—"Granny didn't kill Ruthie. She was with Doc Clyde."

"Don't you think that the intruder today might be our killer?" Jack Henry asked a very good question.

I had been so wrapped up in proving that Granny didn't do it that I didn't place the intruder.

"Vernon, I'm asking you to keep this between us." Jack Henry gestured to my head. "Official police business that I'm not ready to let the public know just yet."

Vernon nodded.

"And I don't want the community to feel threatened."

Vernon continued to nod and let himself out.

Jack Henry waited until we heard the basement door before he turned back to me. "One thing we do know is that this person has overalls."

"I was trying to grab the mask." I went over to the office closet when I noticed the door was ajar. I opened it and found Earl's tin box had been rummaged through and the picture had been taken out of the frame and ripped into pieces. I bent down. Picking up the pieces, I let them fall through my fingers.

"What is all of that?" Jack Henry stood over me.

"It was nothing, but I'm beginning to think it's evidence." The ring was gone, but the other junky stuff was still there. I reached into my pocket and pulled out the snapshot I had stuck in there before I went to see Cheryl Lynne. "They didn't get this."

I held it up over my head and gave it to Jack Henry. As he inspected it, I got up and went to the bathroom to wash the blood out of my hair before it dried.

"That is the same picture as the one that is in pieces," I yelled over the running faucet. I picked and pulled the blood from my hair. The new highlights weren't looking so good. "It's Earl Way's family. Look at the back."

I took the towel and gently rubbed my wet hair on my way back in the office.

Jack Henry was sitting in my chair, writing in his notebook.

"I'm writing all the names down and going to check this out." He didn't look up. "They were looking for something. What else was in that box?"

He jotted more notes as I described the fancy ring. "There was a ruby missing from the bottom of the shield on the ring." Not that we were ever going to find the gem, but like Jack Henry would say, *no stone unturned.* "I'm glad you came by when you did."

"Oh, yeah." He glanced up and with a crooked smile he said, "The mayor called and told me that someone saw you talking to yourself at Higher

Grounds. Since she knew we were friends, she thought she'd tell me to check on you."

"That was nice of her." I laughed. "I did try to act a little cuckoo on purpose."

I didn't go into detail because I could tell Jack Henry really got me. He was probably the only person other than my parents who truly understood me.

"And she said that Hettie Bell was close to getting all of those signatures."

"No way!" I gasped.

"Yep." He stood up. Holding the edge of the picture, he shook it at me. "I'm taking this back to the station and I'm going to put all of these names in the database to see what I come up with."

"As far as I know, Earl didn't have a next of kin." I recalled his funeral. "That is probably why Earl left the inn and everything else to Granny."

"Someone knows something." He pointed to the picture. "The same someone running around here has the same overalls that these people do."

"I think that you should check out Beulah again. I think she was attacked from the front." I didn't give him my source. He didn't say anything, just made a note in his little notebook.

I glanced out the window. The curtain rod dangled off the hinge from where I had pulled down the curtains. John Howard would be able to fix those for me.

"You stay put. Lock the doors and don't let anyone in." Jack Henry gave me orders before he left.

Little did he know how stubborn I was.

Chapter 25

Slicklizzard.

The small wooden-plank sign was driven into the ground.

"I guess we are here." I zoomed past the sign, glad I didn't blink.

Slicklizzard was so far off the beaten path, the map on my phone didn't even pick it up when I typed it in.

"Earl never took me here." Ruthie looked out the window. There was sadness in her voice.

"Ruthie"—I reached over to give her some comfort—"that doesn't matter. All that matters is we figure out who did this to you. Besides, you had some nice dates with Vernon Baxter."

There was no way I was going to agree with Ruthie. Earl loved Granny. There was no denying it.

"Vernon was fun." Ruthie smiled, glancing out the window. "He liked to play Scrabble."

I let Ruthie bask in her memories as I pulled into the only restaurant I saw.

Spare Time Country Cooking.

"I'm going to go in and ask for directions to the courthouse." I looked in the rearview mirror and made sure the stitches were covered over with my hair. I opened the car door and got out.

Ruthie wasn't going to let me go alone, she followed right alongside.

"Take a seat, darlin'." The woman behind the counter casually looked at me as she managed to clean off a couple of tables. "You need a menu?"

"No, I'm looking for directions." I stepped into the tiny restaurant, noticing that the men at the bar had rotated their stools around to look at me.

Old tin signs hung on the wall, giving the feel of a cozy Southern diner.

"You are lucky we are here." One of the old men at the bar twirled back around to face the kitchen area. "We were about to leave after this last cup of coffee."

"Great!" I smiled and walked up to the one

empty stool. I plopped my purse on the counter. "I'll take a cup too."

"Shirley, put on another cup of coffee in your spare time!" he hollered.

The waitress that greeted us sauntered behind the counter and switched out the coffee filters.

"Bobby Poor." He held out his dry thick hand for me to shake. "I named the place Spare Time because it reflects how often I'm open. In my spare time."

"Oh." I smiled at his way of thinking. "Very clever."

"Me and my boys come here every morning." He looked down the bar stools at the other older men. "Ain't that right, boys?"

They all nodded. One John Deere cap after another.

"Where you going?"

"I'm looking for someone related to the Payne family from Slicklizzard." I thanked Shirley when she sat the fresh cup of coffee in front of me. I reached over to grab a couple creamer packets from the small brown bowl.

"You are the third person who has come in here asking about the Paynes in the last couple of days." Shirley searched me like I had a plausible explanation.

"Really?" I was sure one of them had to be Jack Henry since he was investigating Ruthie, but who was the other?

"Just yesterday a pretty young thing came in here claiming to be Earl Way Payne's grand-daughter," Bobby Poor said.

"Granddaughter?" Ruthie got real close to Bobby. "Earl didn't have any son or daughter to have a granddaughter."

"I didn't think Earl Way had any kids himself." I continued the conversation, trying not to give anything away.

"Listen here." Bobby Poor's voice broke with a husky tone. "You tell me why you are here and asking so many questions about Earl Way. Can't anyone die in peace nowadays?"

"It wasn't like he had anything to leave behind." Shirley washed the mugs in hot, soapy water in the sink behind the counter. "His theory was spend it while you were alive." She laughed. "I remember him saying, Shirley, can't take it with you. Have you ever seen a U-haul behind a hearse?"

All the men laughed but Bobby Poor. He was waiting for my answer.

"I'm his step-granddaughter, Emma Lee Raines." I nodded.

"You Zula's granddaughter!" He smacked me

on the back. "We love when she comes to visit. Earl brought her here a time or two."

"Oh . . . !" Ruthie called out, holding her heart. "He did love her more! I don't care if I never cross over to see him again!" She disappeared into thin air.

"I am and Granny is in a bit of trouble." I explained over another cup of coffee about Ruthie's death, but left out the ghost part. "I have to prove she didn't kill Ruthie."

"We knew that girl wasn't his granddaughter, so we told her we didn't know nothing about Earl Way, but he left here with his sister and never came back," Bobby said.

"Sister?" I asked.

I didn't think he had a sister, but I guess one of the people in the photo might've been his sister. I thought they were cousins.

"Oh, yeah." Bobby nodded. "He has a sister. Bless her heart." He shook his head and frowned. "She looked just like him with all that crazy hair. She was a bit . . . odd."

Crazy hair? Odd? The people in the photo had crazy hair just like the camper that Cheryl Lynne and John Howard had seen at three A.M. Was Earl's sister back and on a rampage?

"Thanks," I took some cash out of my purse

and put it on the counter. I had to get back to Sleepy Hollow and let Jack Henry know that Earl Way had a sister and she could be disguised as a camper.

"Oh, that girl that came in." Shirley stopped me on the way out. "She had some sort of red stone and said something about a ring that might have been pawned. A Payne family ring. But we didn't know what she was talking about. We don't have a pawn shop in Slicklizzard."

Ring?

"Thank you!" I screamed, and rushed out the door.

"Did you know his sister?" I asked Ruthie once we were back in the hearse and headed back to Sleepy Hollow.

"Never." She shook her head. There was disappointment all over her face. "You can ask Zula about it. I'm sure she knows."

Ruthie sat in silence the entire way back, which was fine with me since I was trying to process everything Shirley and Bobby Poor had told me.

Chapter 26

I had to get the tin box out of my office closet and give it to Jack Henry. Somehow he was going to have to get a warrant to search Hettie's property.

I whipped around the country roads as fast as the hearse would take me; unfortunately it wasn't as fast as I wanted it to be. That was the one thing with funeral coaches. They weren't meant for fast road driving. There was no reason for a hearse to ever go fast, after all, the dead weren't going anywhere quick.

I reached into my bag and dialed Jack Henry's number. There was no time to track him down. He had to meet me at Eternal Slumber.

"It's me, Emma," I said into the answering machine like he didn't know who I was. The phone chirped, signaling it was about to die. "I've got something big to tell you. Or maybe you already know. I think Hettie Bell is the killer. I know Hettie Bell is the killer. Meet me at the inn."

I threw the phone on the seat and with two hands gripping the wheel, I prayed that we could stop Hettie from doing anything too brash. My first concern was Granny. I had to get her to safety. And my second concern was the time frame.

If Hettie did get the signatures, she would be presenting them to the council anytime now. And if she didn't get the signatures . . . I didn't want to even think about what she'd do to Granny.

I reached over to get my phone. It would probably be a good idea to call Granny to give her a heads-up.

"Crap." I threw it back down. I had forgotten to charge it last night—well, I forgot a lot of stuff that went on last night.

Why was it when you were in a hurry to get somewhere that it seemed to take forever to get there? The inn was dark. The mountainous backdrop did a great job shielding the building from the burning sun, making it darker in the evenings, way before dusk.

Still, there weren't any guests in the rocking chairs on the front porch and it was about dinnertime.

Cars lined the street and around the corner toward the courthouse, which told me that the council meeting must be taking place.

The hearse barely fit in the only spot in the inn's gravel lot. I threw it in park and jumped out, heading up the stairs.

"Granny?" I yelled into each room as I popped my head in. There wasn't a sound anywhere. "Granny?"

Thump, thump, thump. The noise above my head caught my attention.

I bolted up the stairs into Granny's room, but she wasn't there.

Thump, thump, thump.

Fear knotted in my stomach. The noise was coming from the creepy attic.

I tiptoed down the hall because it seemed way too quiet for me. I reached for the attic door handle, but pulled away. The noise got louder and without thinking I flung the door open and ran up the steps.

Sunlight was coming through the old dirty attic windows, just enough to see Hettie tied up in the far back corner.

"Hettie!" I screamed. Making sure I kept my feet on the attic boards, I raced back there to help her.

"Stop right there," a familiar voice called out to me. "I will shoot."

Apparently, the person wasn't kidding. Hettie's eyes grew two sizes and nearly fell out of her head. I could even see her throat make a big gulp.

Click. That was all I needed to hear before I threw my hands up in the air.

"Turn around." *Click.* "Slowly."

I did exactly what I was told to do. Then I came face-to-face with Mayor May and her gun, which was pointed straight at me.

"If you don't mind." She reached around and pulled something out of her overalls' back pocket and threw it at me. "Take that rope and be a dear by wrapping yourself good and tight right over there by Hettie."

Mayor May?

All of the clues I had gathered filled my head.

"Fine." I backed up toward Hettie and eased myself down next to her. The little bit of streaming light let me see that Hettie's mouth had been gagged.

"Be sure to get it nice and tight so I can tie you up like the little hogs I did when I was a kid." She swung the gun in front of her.

The attic was so humid, it was hard for me to

breathe. It was hard to concentrate on what she was saying.

"Are you okay?" Mayor May asked as if she really cared. Her perfectly done makeup was starting to drip from the humid air, and her long hair was starting to kink up.

"I'm . . ." I gasped. Mayor May looked exactly like one of the people in the picture. "You killed Ruthie."

Ruthie appeared, sort of floating above the mayor. She looked like she was about to spit nails.

"Shut up!"

"And you hurt Beulah." My mouth was spewing like a volcano. If I was going to die, I was going to solve Ruthie's murder if it was the last thing I did on this earth. "Why?"

"Not like I owe you an explanation, but I am a genius." She glowed in her own brilliance. "I am going to be governor of this great state and no one, not even a little inn like this one or my brother's lovers are going to keep me from it."

"Brother?"

"Earl Way Payne was my brother. Before he died, he knew we were going to sell the inn in order to get a development company in here and grow the community." She waved the gun around. "It will look good for my platform when I get elected."

"But why kill Ruthie?"

"She was standing in my way. Even Zula knew a good thing when she saw it." She grinned; her eyes looked like the devil. "Only I can't count on Zula. So I intercepted her little tax payments over the past few years and secretly tied into her bank accounts. Behind bars was a safe place for Zula. I didn't want to kill her. She had always been so kind."

I took the rope and wrapped it around my ankles, trying to take my time. Surely Jack Henry would be there any minute, do some big police standoff, and save us.

"Everything was coming together until little miss priss over there decided to stick her nose into everything." Mayor May jabbed the gun toward Hettie. "She had to be the hero and get all of those signatures. I wasn't about to let this deal go south. My political career depended on making Sleepy Hollow Kentucky's number-one tourist destination."

Hettie squirmed, trying to get away.

The last bit of daylight shined through the window and put a spotlight on the gun. I followed the barrel to Mayor May's hand. She gripped it firmly in her right hand.

"Your ring!" I blurted out and accidently dropped the rope when I went weak.

"I told you it was a ring!" Ruthie stood next to Mayor May with her hands on her hips, tapping her kitty slippers.

"It's a family ring, idiot." Sarcasm dripped from her bare lips. Her bright red lipstick had melted down her chin. Mayor May was suddenly not looking so pretty. "I knew I had to get rid of old Ruthie Sue when she baited me with the framed picture of our family. I know she was going to use that to uncover my past. Then I would've never made it to the governor's office."

"I saw that picture in an antique shop in Lexington." Ruthie shook her finger at Mayor May. "Tell her that it spoke to me. I had no idea it was my Earl's family!"

I didn't dare talk to Ruthie. I tried really hard to concentrate on one conversation at a time, especially since a gun was pointed at me.

The humidity had caused all the Mayor's makeup to melt off and her hair was tight and curly up to her chin.

"Beulah is still hanging on, but I'll take care of her. It was priceless, you all drunk doing who knows what with Jack Henry Ross, when you told him you were going to get Beulah for spreading rumors." Mayor May's nose flared, and then a look of satisfaction flickered in her eyes. "I just so happened to be across the street and heard it all. I couldn't let the opportunity slip by me. Zula for tax evasion, you for murder. Perfect."

"Why?" I questioned her. I still didn't understand why she needed to go to such extremes. "Especially now that you are going to kill your own family."

"I have no other family," she said through gritted teeth. She opened her mouth to say something else, but the humidity must've gotten to her veneers. They popped right out and landed on the attic floor, crashing into tiny bright white pieces. "This is not going as planned!" She screamed, "Hurry up! Tie your knees!"

"Hettie is related to you somehow!" I blurted out. "Tell her Hettie!"

Mayor May jerked the gag out of Hettie's mouth.

"I am your niece from your sister, Pearl." Hettie spoke softly.

"Pearl died during childbirth, you fool!" Mayor May wiggled the gun in the air. "You are pathetic, trying to come here and take what Earl Way built up and is mine!"

"I am that child. I was put up for adoption by my biological father, who has now died. I'm not trying to take anyone's fortune. I'm only trying to have a family. Please don't kill me." Hettie's head dropped as big sobs left her mouth, her body heaving up and down.

I was going to reach over and console her but grabbed her instead, taking her to the floor when I saw Jack Henry rush up the stairs, point his gun and fire.

"Argh!" Mayor May's gun flew in the air. She went down to her knees, holding her hand.

I scrambled on my knees to get the loose gun. The rope easily fell off. I reached out and grabbed the gun, just as Mayor May sat up holding her hand to her chest. She grimaced with pain.

"I can take over from here." Jack Henry never took his gun off of the mayor. He eased over to me and took the gun. "Help Hettie out of here."

Quickly I untied Hettie and did what he said. Other officers had already gotten there and secured the scene.

When we got safely outside, I saw Granny coming down the street away from the courthouse, followed by the rest of the council and community members.

"How did you find out about me being a Payne?" Hettie rubbed her wrists where the mayor had hog-tied her. There were deep indents in her skin.

"I followed you to the records room and found

out you were researching the Paynes. Then I went to Slicklizzard and the Spare Time."

She grinned. "The old geezers told you I stopped in there."

"Yea, but I thought you were the killer when Shirley told me you had a stone that went with the ring from Earl's tin box I found in the attic." I couldn't help but smile as Granny got closer, her arms flailing in the air. "I was sure you were the killer."

"I just wanted to do right by Earl." She shrugged. "But if he wanted to sell the inn like the mayor said, I guess I wasn't doing any favors by tracking down the family and then doing the petition."

She reached around and pulled some papers out of her back pocket. She handed them to me.

"I was on my way to the council meeting when I got a message from the mayor to meet her at the inn. That was when she grabbed me." There were tears gathering on the rims of her eyelids. "I had no idea she was my aunt."

"Where have you been all this time?"

"My biological mother died during childbirth and I was adopted." She dabbed her eyes before she pulled out the ring with the missing stone. "I traced my heritage here. I didn't know Mayor May was my aunt until her hair went all crazy and her fake teeth fell out up there."

We both broke out in laughter.

"What is going on?" Granny hustled over to us and she pointed to all the police cruisers with their lights flashing. Doc Clyde wasn't too far behind her.

I gave him the wonky eye and briefly filled her in on what was going on.

"Clyde, get over here and check her out." She gestured for Doc Clyde to come over.

"I'm fine." I waved him away. "I know about you two by the way." I pointed one to the other.

Granny paid no attention to my comment. A sure sign she wasn't ready to acknowledge to the world that they were a couple. Like a good Southern girl, I kept my mouth closed and didn't pressure her to tell me.

After Granny gave me the once-over, she excused herself and went into the inn.

Shortly thereafter, Jack Henry brought Mayor May out in cuffs. Her right hand was bandaged, she looked befuddled and didn't look like the mayor who Sleepy Hollow had elected.

"I'm going to be Governor one day!" Mayor May screeched and tried to tug away as the cop hoisted her up from behind with her cuffed wrists. "Then I'm going to grant myself a pardon!"

The Mayor glanced over and kept her eye focused on me. Her crazy curly hair was sticking up all over the place and her mouth was mumbling something that was not so nice toward me, exposing her gritty teeth.

"Have a nice time." I winked and waved the way she taught the good citizens of Sleepy Hollow. Jack Henry eased her into the back of a cruiser, then patted the trunk of the car, which gave the signal for the police officer to take off with the lights twirling and the sirens blaring.

"That's what you get when you spend your entire life lying and on the wrong side of the law." Jack Henry pointed toward the cruiser speeding off toward the county jail. He called one of the EMTs over. "Can you please take Hettie to the hospital so she can get checked out?"

Hettie let the paramedic put her in an ambulance to take her to a Lexington area hospital.

"I'm so glad you are okay." Jack Henry wrapped his strong arms around me, holding me close. "When I got your message, I was scared."

Those were the sweetest words I had ever heard. I relaxed, letting my body mold into his.

"I got the autopsy back and put two-and–two together about the ring." He rubbed my back. "I got a warrant to search Hettie's apartment and found a ruby matching the one you described. I was sure it was her, but I remembered how much the mayor was getting on me to solve the crime and then I remembered how you said you saw her at the salon."

He was rattling off all the clues I had found and never once put them together like he did.

"I asked Mary Anna about the mayor and she described her hair." He let go of me and pulled out the snapshot. "Once I heard Mary Anna's description, I knew this picture was the mayor. I just knew it. That was when I got your message. I rushed over because I had stopped by the meeting and neither the mayor nor Hettie was there. I smelled trouble and called for backup."

A couple of the officers came over to get some signatures from Jack Henry, not giving me any time to properly thank him.

"Can you come down to the station and give a detailed account of what happened?" Jack Henry asked.

"Of course." I put a finger up when I saw Ruthie standing next to the hearse. "I need a minute though."

Jack Henry didn't question me. It was like he knew what I was going to do.

Chapter 27

"You did good, kiddo." Ruthie sat in the passenger side of the hearse and looked over all of the hubbub going on around the inn.

"Thanks," I whispered, glancing down at my hands in my lap. All of the windows were rolled up and I had the radio playing so if anyone saw me talking to myself, they would think I was singing . . . maybe. "I couldn't have done it without you."

"I can't wait to get my hands on one Earl Way Payne when I get up there." She was as mad as a hornet. She looked up to the sky and shook an angry fist. "Never once did he take me to Slicklizzard or tell me about his sister." She crossed her arms.

"Don't be too hard on him." My eyes felt a stinging sensation creeping up. I tried not to blink, but couldn't help it. A tear ran down my cheek.

Ruthie reached over and tried to catch it, but it went right through her hand and into my lap.

"Don't cry." Ruthie reached over and touched me, only it was much lighter than it had been in the past few days. I was losing her to the great beyond little by little. "I'll be sure to keep an eye on you from above."

"Ha ha! You better." I smiled and looked at my sidekick. Panic bubbled in my gut, and my throat tightened. "Ruthie? Where are you?"

A bright light bolted out of the sky and suddenly vanished.

Just like that. She was gone.

Ruthie Sue Payne might have been a pain, but she was my pain.

Without a good-bye, she slipped out of my life.

Chapter 28

*B*ang, bang, bang.
"Hold on!" I screamed. I wiggled out from my comfy cocoon, where I had been for the twenty-four hours since Ruthie left.

It was as if she had died all over again, only this time I felt she'd been a real friend and not some grumpy, gossipy old bag from the Auxiliary.

The sun was shining through the glass on my private entrance door. I knew I was going to have to face life sooner or later. The phone had been ringing off the hook in the office of Eternal Slumber, which meant we were back in business.

"John Howard, what are you doing here?" I propped the door open and held my hand over my eyes to block the sun.

"Miss Emma Lee, I've made an awful mistake." He took his cap off and held it in front of him while he looked down at his shuffling feet.

Instantly, I knew exactly what he wanted. His job back.

"No you didn't." I reached out and grabbed his hands. "You are family and you can come and go as you wish. You will always have a place at Eternal Slumber."

"Thank you. You won't regret it." He placed his cap back on his head and did a little giddy-up before he started down the private entrance stairs.

"Whoa!" Jack Henry called as John Howard almost ran into him when they passed on the steps. "How you doing, John Howard?"

John Howard mumbled a few words that I couldn't hear and they shook hands, parting ways.

"What are you doing here?" I leaned up against the door. I didn't bother trying to fix my hair or rub the makeup off from under my eyes.

The investigation was over and so was the little romance that Jack Henry created between us to keep me feeding him information.

"I came to get you." He had on regular clothes which meant he probably wasn't taking me down for questioning. "We are going to head into Lexington and go see that medium lady I was telling you about."

"Jack." It was time to let him off the hook. "Really, you don't have to pretend to be my date any longer. Ruthie has officially passed over. She's gone."

"I figured as much." He reached over. Taking my hands in his, he gently squeezed them. "I called several times and finally got Charlotte. She said that you were taking a mental health day because of all the trauma."

"She did?" I never told Charlotte anything about a mental health day.

"She must think you need to recover from the crazy mayor and all." His gazed shifted to my eyes. He studied me with curious intensity. "You are okay, right?"

"Yeah. I'm fine." There was still a deep sadness that lingered in my heart. "But you don't have to pretend anymore." I pulled my hands away. "I get it. Really."

"You get that I do want to date you?" A smile ruffled his mouth. "I do remember spin the bottle."

"You do?"

"Yea. I had such a crush on you that when it landed on you, I freaked out." He turned a vivid scarlet. "I was so embarrassed that I played it off and ended up hurting us both."

I felt my pulse suddenly leap with excitement. Was my dream of dating Jack Henry, after all of these years, finally coming true?

"No you didn't." I tried to play coy, but I knew the smile on my face gave me away.

"You are enjoying this little game of groveling, aren't you Emma Lee?" His eyes teased me.

"We were kids." I brushed it off.

"We aren't now and I still have those same feelings." He reached his strong arms around my waist and pulled me closer. "What if we give this a go?"

Jack Henry didn't wait for me to answer. He lowered his head, laying his lips on mine, sending the pit of my stomach into a swirl. After a moment he pulled away.

"Sealed with a kiss." I could still feel the warmth of his lips, but knew more would have to wait until later. After all, we were standing smack-dab in the middle of Sleepy Hollow, where this news was going to be front page. "So what about this medium?"

I had no choice but to go with him. After all, he *was* my boyfriend and had my best interest at heart.

Next thing I knew, I was dressed and we were in the car on our way to Lexington.

We talked so much that I didn't realize the forty minutes and windy roads were long behind us when we pulled up to a small brick house with a tiny porch on the front. No sign, no beads, no strange anything that I would think a medium would have.

"This is it?" I glanced out the window, almost afraid to go in since it looked so normal.

"This is it," he repeated with confidence. "Let's go."

Jack Henry jumped out of the car and rushed around to the passenger side. Like a good gentleman, he opened the door and helped me out.

"I forgot to tell you." There was some excitement fluttering in his eyes. "Beulah Bellefry came to and she identified the ugly mayor as the assailant. You were right, she was attacked from the front."

I wasn't right, Ruthie was, I wanted to tell him, but what was the point? Ruthie was long gone and I bet Earl Way Payne was still taking a beating from her.

We knocked on the door.

"May I help you?" A little boy knee high to a june bug answered the door and had the sweetest Southern accent.

"We are here to see Debbie Dually," Jack Henry told the boy.

"Mama, someone's here to see you!" he hollered.

"Tell them to come in!" a woman yelled back.

"Come on in. I'm David Dually." He grinned, exposing a lost front tooth. "I'm in second grade. Take a seat." He pointed to a glass-top kitchen table in the dining room to the left of the front door.

We did what David Dually told us to do. The table was lit up with all sorts of candles.

Debbie Dually walked around the room without greeting us, but fanning us with some sort of incense by waving a feather in the smoke. She stood all of five feet, with a short brown bob that was neatly curled under her chin. Her bangs were blunt and hit right at her eyebrows.

She was very fashionable in a pair of white capri pants, black short-sleeved shirt and black cork-wedged heels.

"You must be Emma Lee Raines." Her brown eyes twinkled when she said my name. She held her hands out over the table right in front of me. I took them in mine. "I've been waiting all day to meet you."

"Thank you," I whispered, not knowing what to say.

"You must be Jack Henry Ross." She didn't let go of my hands, she only squeezed them, and looked at Jack Henry. "You are a good man to do this for her."

"Thank you." Jack Henry was getting good at blushing.

"Now." She sat down and looked around. She bit the outer corner of her lip. "Who is it that has hot-pink pajamas, kitty slippers, bunch of dangling jewelry and a hair cap?"

"Ruthie," Jack Henry and I said in unison.

"Ruthie is here and she told me to tell you that she took care of Earl." Debbie Dually shrugged and smiled. "She's a sassy one."

"You have no idea." I laughed. That made me feel good that she saw Ruthie and that Ruthie was okay.

"I also have to tell you that you are a Betweener medium." Her words rang in my ear.

"A . . . be . . . what?" I leaned in with my mouth dropped open.

"A Betweener." She waved her hand to and fro. "They are the dead that are sort of stuck in the here and there." She pointed to the sky. "Most of the time they have some unfinished business to take care of. In your case," she paused as if she were looking for the right words, "most of them will have been . . . offed."

"Offed?"

"You know." She wiggled her nose. "Murdered."

"Murdered?" I jumped up. "No! No way!" I wiggled back at her. No way on this green earth was I going to help solve anyone else's murder. One was enough.

"Ruthie said you weren't going to like it." She wrote a few things down on a little notepad.

What was it with people and notepads?

"You will do great things, Emma Lee Raines." Debbie Dually drummed her long fingernails on the glass-top table, sending beads of sweat to gather on my forehead.

I didn't want any part of this.

"Is that it?" She eyed me. "I know it is a lot to take in, but I also know we will meet again."

"Thank you," I whispered and stood up, signaling to Jack Henry that it was time to go.

Jack Henry and I left in dead silence. I didn't know if it was because he was trying to process what she had told me or if I was trying to process what she had told me. All I know is that Chicken Teater stood by the car when we walked out.

"Emma Lee?" Chicken Teater stood six-foot-two in his bare feet, red plaid shirt and carpenter jeans. His hair had always stayed combed to the right side as far as I could remember. He was one of my daddy's friends, who pretty much kept to himself and was one of the first bodies I had ever laid to rest . . . or so I had thought. "Emma Lee, I know you can hear and see me."

"This is not happening. This is not happening," I murmured.

"I'm sure no one is ever going to contact you again," Jack Henry assured me and opened the passenger door. "Don't worry about it."

I gulped and smiled before I got in. He shut the door and went to get in the driver's seat.

"Ruthie Sue Payne sent me." Chicken Teater confirmed it. Ruthie Sue Payne really was going to be a pain.

Just think, this all started because of Santa Claus. I took a drink of my large Diet Coke Big Gulp that I had picked up from the Buy and Fly gas station on the way over to Sleepy Hollow Cemetery to watch Chicken Teater's body being exhumed from his eternal resting place—only he was far from restful.

Damn Santa. I sucked up a mouthful of Diet Coke and swallowed. *Damn Santa.*

No, I didn't mean the real jolly guy with the belly shaking like a bowlful of jelly who leaves baby dolls and toy trucks; I meant the plastic light-up ornamental kind that people stick in their front yards during Christmas. The particular plastic Santa I was talking about was the one that had fallen off the roof of Artie's Deli and Meat just as I happened to walk under it, knocking me out cold.

Santa didn't give me anything but a bump on the head and the gift of seeing ghosts—let me be more specific—ghosts of people who have been murdered. They called me the Betweener, at least that was what the psychic from Lexington told us . . . *us* . . . *sigh* . . . I looked over at Jack Henry.

The Ray Ban sunglasses covered up his big brown eyes, which were the exact same color as a Hershey's chocolate bar. I was a goner. Lost, in fact.

Today I was positive his eyes would be watering from the stench of a casket that had been buried for four years—almost four years to the day, now that I thought about it.

Jack Henry, my boyfriend and Sleepy Hollow sheriff, motioned for John Howard Lloyd to drop the claw that was attached to the tractor and begin digging. John Howard, my employee at Eternal Slumber Funeral Home, didn't mind digging up the grave. He dug it four years ago, so why not? He hummed a tune, happily chewing—gumming, since he had no teeth—a piece of straw he had grabbed up off the ground before he took his post behind the tractor controls. If someone who didn't know him came upon John Howard, they'd think he was a serial killer, with his dirty overalls, wiry hair and gummy smile.

The buzz of a moped scooter caused me to look

back at the street. There was a crowd that had gathered behind the yellow police line to see what was happening because it wasn't every day someone's body was plucked from its resting place.

"Zula Fae Raines Payne, get back here!" an officer scolded my Granny, who didn't pay him any attention. She waved her handkerchief in the air with one hand while she steered her moped right on through the police tape. "This is a crime scene and you aren't allowed over there."

Granny didn't even wobble but held the moped steady when she snapped right through the yellow tape.

"Woo hoooo, Emma!" Granny hollered, ignoring the officer, who was getting a little too close to her. A black helmet snapped on the side covered the top of her head, giving her plenty of room to sport her large black-rimmed sunglasses. She twisted the handle to full throttle. The officer took off at a full sprint to catch up to her. He put his arm out to grab her. "I declare!" Granny jerked her head back. "I'm Zula Raines Payne, the owner of Eternal Slumber, and this is one of my clients!"

"Ma'am, I know who you are. With all due respect, because my momma and pa taught me to respect my elders—and I do respect you, Ms. Payne—I can't let you cross that tape. You are going to have to go back behind the line!" He ran behind her and pointed to the yellow tape that she had already zipped through. "This is a crime scene. Need I remind you that you turned over operations of your business to your granddaughter? And only *she* has the right to be on the other side of the line."

I curled my head back around to see what Jack Henry and John were doing and pretended the roar of the excavator was drowning out the sounds around me, including those of Granny screaming my name. Plus, I didn't want to get into any sort of argument with Granny, since half the town came out to watch the 7 A.M. exhumation, and the Auxiliary women were the first in line—and would be the first at the Higher Grounds Café, eating their scones, drinking their coffee and coming up with all sorts of reasons why we had exhumed the body.

I could hear them now. *"Ever since Zula Fae left Emma Lee and Charlotte Rae in charge of Eternal Slumber, it's gone downhill"* or my personal favorite, *"I'm not going to lay my corpse at Eternal Slumber just to have that crazy Emma Lee dig me back up. Especially since she's got a case of the Funeral Trauma."*

The "Funeral Trauma." After the whole Santa incident, I told Doc Clyde I was having some sort of hallucinations and seeing dead people. He said I had been in the funeral business a little too long and seeing corpses all of my life had been traumatic.

Regardless, the officer was half right—me and my

sister were in charge of Eternal Slumber. At twenty-eight, I had been an undertaker for only three years. But I had been around the funeral home my whole life. It is the family business, one I didn't want to do until I turned twenty-five years old and decided I better keep the business going. *Some business*. Currently, Granny still owned Eternal Slumber, but my sister, Charlotte Rae, and I ran the joint.

My parents completely retired and moved to Florida. Thank God for Skype or I'd never see them. I guess Granny was semi-retired. I say semi-retired because she put her two cents in when she wanted to. Today she wanted to.

Some family business.

Granny brought the moped to an abrupt stop. She hopped right off and flicked the snap of the strap and pulled the helmet off along with her sunglasses. She hung the helmet on the handlebars and the glasses dangled from the *V* in her sweater exactly where she wanted it to hang—between her boobs. Doc Clyde was there and Granny had him on the hook exactly where she wanted to keep him.

Her short red hair looked like it was on fire, with the morning sun beaming down, as she used her fingers to spike it up a little more than usual. After all, she knew she had to look good because she was center of attention—next to Chicken Teater's exhumed body.

The officer ran up and grabbed the scooter's handle. He knew better than to touch Granny.

"I am sure your momma and paw did bring you up right, but if you don't let me go . . ." Granny jerked the scooter toward her. She was a true Southern belle and put things in a way that no other woman could. I looked back at them and waved her over. The police officer stepped aside. Granny took her hanky out of her bra and wiped off the officer's shoulder like she was cleaning lint or something. "It was *lovely* to meet you," Granny's voice dripped like sweet honey. She put the hanky back where she had gotten it.

I snickered. Lovely wasn't always a compliment from a Southern gal. Like the gentleman he claimed to be, he took his hat off to Granny and smiled.

She didn't pay him any attention as she bee-lined it toward me.

"Hi," she said in her sweet Southern drawl, waving at everyone around us. She gave a little extra wink toward Doc Clyde. His cheeks rose to a scarlet red. Nervously, he ran his fingers through his thinning hair and pushed it to the side, defining the side part.

Everyone in town knew he had been keeping late hours just for Granny, even though she wasn't a bit sick. God knew what they were doing and I didn't want to know.

Granny pointed her hanky toward Pastor Brown, who was there to say a little prayer when the casket was exhumed. Waking the dead wasn't high on anyone's priority list. Granny put the cloth over her mouth, and leaning in, she whispered, "Emma Lee, you better have a good reason to be digging up Chicken Teater."

We both looked at the concrete chicken gravestone, which stood seven feet high. The small gold plate at the base of the stone statue displayed all of Colonel Chicken Teater's stats, with his parting words: *Chicken has left the coop.*

"Why don't you go worry about the inn," I suggested for her to leave and glanced over at John Howard. He had to be getting close to reaching the casket vault.

Granny gave me the stink eye.

"It was only a suggestion." I put my hands up in the air as a truce sign.

Granny owned, operated and lived at the only bed-and-breakfast in town, the Sleepy Hollow Inn, known as "the Inn" around here. Everyone loved staying at the large mansion, which sat at the foothills of the caverns and caves that made Sleepy Hollow a main attraction in Kentucky . . . besides horses and University of Kentucky basketball.

Sleepy Hollow was a small tourist town that was low on crime, and that was the way we liked it.

Sniff, sniff. Whimpers were coming from underneath a large black floppy hat.

Granny and I looked over at Marla Maria Teater, Chicken's wife. She had come dressed to the nines, with her black V-neck dress hitting her curves in all the right places. The hat covered up the eyes she was dabbing.

Of course, when the police notified her that they had good reason to believe that Chicken didn't die of a serious bout of pneumonia but was murdered, Marla took to her bed as any mourning widower would. She insisted on being here for the exhumation. Jack Henry had warned Marla Maria to keep quiet about why the police were opening up the files on Chicken's death. If there was a murderer on the loose and it got around, it could possibly hurt the economy, and this was Sleepy Hollow's busiest time of the year.

Granny put her arm around Marla and winked at me over Marla's shoulder.

"Now, now. I know it's hard, honey, I've buried a few myself. Granted, I've never had any dug up though." Granny wasn't lying. She has been twice widowed and I was hoping she'd stay away from marriage a third time. Poor Doc Clyde, you'd have thought he would stay away from her since her track record was . . . well . . . deadly. "That's a first in this town." Granny gave Marla Maria the elbow along with a wink and a click of her tongue.

Maybe the third time was the charm.

"Who is buried here?" Granny let go of Marla and stepped over to the smaller tombstone right next to Chicken's.

"Stop!" Jack Henry screamed, waving his hands in the air. "Zula, move!"

Granny looked up and ducked just as John Howard came back for another bite of ground with the claw.

I would hate to have to bury Granny anytime soon.

"Lady Cluckington," Marla whispered, tilting her head to the side. Using her finger, she dabbed the driest eyes I had ever seen. "Our prize chicken. Well, she isn't dead *yet*."

I glanced over at her. Her tone caused a little suspicion to stir in my gut.

"She's not a chicken. She's a Spangled Russian Orloff Hen!" Chicken Teater appeared next to his grave. His stone looked small next to his six-foot-two frame. He ran his hand over the tombstone Granny had asked about. There was a date of birth, but no date of death. "You couldn't stand having another beauty queen in my life!"

"Oh no," I groaned and took another gulp of my Diet Coke. He—his ghost—was the last thing that I needed to see this morning.

"Is that sweet tea?" Chicken licked his lips. "I'd give anything to have a big ol' sip of sweet tea." He towered over me. His hair was neatly combed to the right; his red plaid shirt was tucked into his carpenter jeans.

This was the third time I had seen Chicken Teater since his death almost four years ago to the day. It was a shock to the community to hear of a man passing from pneumonia in his early sixties. But that was what the doctors in Lexington said he died of, no questions asked, and his funeral was held at Eternal Slumber.

The first time I had seen Chicken Teater's ghost was after my perilous run-in with Santa. I too thought I was a goner, gone to the great beyond . . . but no . . . Chicken Teater and Ruthie Sue Payne—their ghosts anyway—stood right next to my hospital bed, eyeballing me. Chicken gave me the once-over as if he was trying to figure out if I was dead or alive. Lucky for him I was alive and seeing him.

Ruthie Sue Payne was a client at Eternal Slumber who refused to cross over until someone helped her solve her murder. That someone was me. The In-Betweener.

Since I could see her, talk to her, feel her and hear her, I was the one. Thanks to me, Ruthie's murder was solved and she was now resting peacefully on the other side. Chicken was a different story.

Apparently, Ruthie was as big of a gossip in the afterlife as she was in her earthly life. That was how Chicken Teater knew about me being an In-Betweener. Evidently, Ruthie was telling everyone about my special gift.

Chicken Teater wouldn't leave me alone until I agreed to investigate his death because he knew he didn't die from pneumonia. He claimed he was murdered. But who would want to kill a chicken farmer?

Regardless, it took several months of me trying to convince Jack Henry there might be a possibility Chicken Teater was murdered. After some questionable evidence provided by Chicken Teater, the case was reopened. I didn't understand all the red tape and legal yip-yap, but here we stood today.

Now it was time for me to get Chicken Teater to the other side.

"It's not dead yet?" Granny's eyebrows rose in amazement after Marla Maria confirmed there was an empty grave. Granny couldn't get past the fact there was a gravestone for something that wasn't dead.

I was still stuck on "prize chicken." What was a prize chicken?

A loud thud echoed when John Howard sent the claw down. There was an audible gasp from the crowd. The air was thick with anticipation. What did they think they were going to see?

Suddenly my nerves took a downward dive. What if the coffin opened? Coffin makers guaranteed they lock for eternity after they are sealed, but still, it wouldn't be a good thing for John Howard to pull the coffin up and have Chicken take a tumble next to Lady Cluckington's stone.

"I think we got 'er!" John Howard stood up in the cab of the digger with pride on his face as he looked down in the hole. "Yep! That's it!" he hollered over the roar of the running motor.

Jack Henry ran over and hooked some cables on the excavator and gave the thumbs-up.

Pastor Brown dipped his head and moved his lips in a silent prayer. Granny nudged me with her boney elbow to bow my head, and I did. Marla Maria cried out.

"Aw shut up!" Chicken Teater told her and smiled as he saw his coffin being raised from the earth. "They are going to figure out who killed me, and so help me if it was you . . ." He shook his fist in the air in Marla Maria's direction.

Curiosity stirred in my bones. Was it going to be easy getting Chicken Teater to the other side? Was Marla Maria Teater behind his death, as Chicken believed?

She was the only one who was not only in his

bed at night, but right by his deathbed, so he told me. I took my little notebook out from my back pocket. I had learned from Ruthie's investigation to never leave home without it. I jotted down what Chicken had said to Marla Maria, with prize chickens next to it, followed up by a lot of exclamation points. Oh . . . I had almost forgotten that Marla Maria was Miss Kentucky in her earlier years—a *beauty queen*—I quickly wrote that down too.

"Are you getting all of this?" Chicken questioned me and twirled his finger in a circle as he referred to the little scene Marla Maria was causing with her meltdown. She leaned her butt up against Lady Cluckington's stone. Chicken rushed over to his prize chicken's gravestone and tried to shove Marla Maria off. "Get your—"

Marla Maria jerked like she could feel something touch her. She shivered. Her body shimmied from her head to her toes.

I cleared my throat, doing my best to get Chicken to stop fussing and cursing. "Are you okay?" I asked. Did she feel him?

Granny stood there taking it all in.

She crossed her arms in front of her and ran her hands up and down them. "I guess when I buried Chicken, I thought that was the end of it. This is creeping me out a little bit."

End of it? End of what? Your little murder plot? My

mind unleashed all sorts of ways Marla Maria might have offed her man. That seemed a little too suspicious for me. Marla buttoned her lip when Jack Henry walked over. More suspicious behavior that I duly noted.

"Can you tell me how he died?" I put a hand on her back to offer some comfort, though I knew she was putting on a good act.

She shook her head, dabbed her eye and said, "He was so sick. Coughing and hacking. I was so mad because I had bags under my eyes from him keeping me up at night." *Sniff, sniff.* "I had to dab some Preparation H underneath my eyes in order to shrink them." She tapped her face right above her cheekbones.

"That's where my butt cream went?" Chicken hooted and hollered. "She knew I had a hemorrhoid the size of a golf ball and she used my cream on her face?" Chicken flailed his arms around in the air.

I bit my lip and stepped a bit closer to Marla Maria so I couldn't see Chicken out of my peripheral vision. There were a lot of things I had heard in my time, but hemorrhoids were something that I didn't care to know about.

I stared at Marla Maria's face. There wasn't a tear, a tear streak, or a single wrinkle on her perfectly made-up face. If hemorrhoids helped shrink her under-eye bags, did it also help shrink her wrinkles?

"Anyway, enough about me." She fanned her face with the handkerchief. "Chicken was so uncomfortable with all the phlegm. He could barely breathe. I let him rest, but called the doctor in the meantime." She nodded and waited for me to agree with her. I nodded back and she continued. "When the doctor came out of the bedroom, he told me Chicken was dead." A cry burst out of her as she threw her head back and held the hanky over her face.

I was sure she was hiding a smile from thinking she was pulling one over on me. Little did she know this wasn't my first rodeo with a murderer. Still, I patted her back while Chicken spat at her feet.

Jack Henry walked over. He didn't take his eyes off of Marla Maria.

"I'm sorry we have to do this, Marla." Jack took his hat off out of respect for the widow. *Black widow*, I thought as I watched her fidget side to side, avoiding all eye contact by dabbing the corners of her eyes. "We are all done here, Zula." He nodded toward Granny.

Granny smiled.

Marla Maria nodded before she turned to go face her waiting public behind the police line.

Granny walked over to say something to Doc

Clyde, giving him a little butt pat making his face even redder than before. I waited until she was out of earshot before I said something to Jack Henry.

"That was weird. Marla Maria is a good actress." I made mention to Jack Henry because sometimes he was clueless as to how women react to different situations.

"Don't be going and blaming her just because she's his wife." Jack Henry was trying to play the good cop he always was, but I wasn't falling for his act. "It's all speculation at this point."

"Wife? She was no kind of wife to me." Chicken kicked his foot in the dirt John Howard had dug from his grave. "She only did one thing as my wife." Chicken looked back and watched Marla Maria play the poor pitiful widow as Beulah Paige Bellefry, president and CEO of Sleepy Hollow's gossip mill, drew her into a big hug while all the other Auxiliary women gathered to put in their two cents.

"La-la-la." I put my fingers in my ears and tried to drown Chicken out. I only wanted to know how he was murdered, not how Marla Maria *was* a wife to him.

"She spent all my money," he cursed under his breath.

"Shoo." I let out an audible sigh.

Over Jack's right shoulder, in the distance some

movement near the trailer park caught my eye. There was a man peering out from behind a tree looking over at all the commotion. His John Deere hat helped shadow his face so I couldn't get a good look, but I chalked it up to being a curious neighbor like the rest of them. Still, I quickly wrote down the odd behavior. I had learned you never know what people knew. And I had to start from scratch on how to get Chicken to the great beyond. I wasn't sure, but I believe Chicken had lived in the trailer park. Maybe the person saw something, maybe not. He was going on the list.

"Are you okay?" Jack pulled off his sunglasses. His big brown eyes were set with worry. I grinned. A smile ruffled his mouth. "Just checking because of the la-la thing." He waved his hands in the air. "I saw you taking some notes and I know what that means."

"Yep." My one word confirmed that Chicken was there and spewing all sorts of valuable information. Jack Henry was the only person who knew I was a Betweener medium, and he knew Chicken was right there with us even though he couldn't see him. When I told him about Chicken Teater's little visits to me and how he wouldn't leave me alone until we figured out who killed him, Jack Henry knew it to be true. "I'll tell you later."

I jotted down a note about Marla Maria spending all of Chicken's money, or so he said. Which made me question her involvement even more. Was he no use to her with a zero bank account and she offed him? I didn't know he had money.

"I can see your little noggin running a mile a minute." Jack bent down and looked at me square in the eyes.

"Just taking it all in." I bit my lip. I had learned from my last ghost that I had to keep some things to myself until I got the full scoop. And right now, Chicken hadn't given me any solid information.

"You worry about getting all the information you can from your little friend." Jack Henry pointed to the air beside me. I pointed to the air beside him where Chicken's ghost was actually standing. Jack grimaced. "Whatever. I don't care where he is." He shivered.

Even though Jack Henry knew I could see ghosts, he wasn't completely comfortable.

"You leave the investigation to me." Jack Henry put his sunglasses back on. Sexy dripped from him, making my heart jump a few beats.

"Uh-huh." I looked away. Looking away from Jack Henry when he was warning me was a common occurrence. I knew I had to do my own investigating and couldn't get lost in his eyes while lying to him.

Besides, I didn't have a whole lot of information.

Chicken knew he was murdered but had no clue how. He was only able to give me clues about his life and it was up to me to put them together.

"I'm not kidding." Jack Henry took his finger and put it on my chin, pulling it toward him. He gave me a quick kiss. "We are almost finished up here. I'll sign all the paperwork and send the body on over to Eternal Slumber for Vernon to get going on some new toxicology reports we have ordered." He took his officer hat off and used his forearm to wipe the sweat off his brow.

"He's there waiting," I said. Vernon Baxter was a retired doctor who performed any and all autopsies the Sleepy Hollow police needed and I let him use Eternal Slumber for free. I had everything a lab would want in the basement of the funeral home.

"Go on up!" Jack Henry gave John the thumbs-up and walked closer. Slowly John Howard lifted the coffin completely out of the grave and sat it right on top of the church truck.

"Do you think she did it?" I glanced over at Marla Maria as she talked a good talk.

"Did what?" Granny walked up and asked. She turned to see what I was looking at. "Did you dig him up because his death is being investigated for murder?" Granny gasped.

"Now Granny, don't go spreading rumors." I couldn't deny or admit to what she said. If I admitted the truth to her question, I would be betraying Jack Henry. If I denied her question, I would have been lying to Granny. And no one lies to Granny.

In a lickety-split, Granny was next to her scooter.

"I'll be over. Put the coffee on," Granny hollered before she put her helmet back on her head, snapped the strap in place, revved up the scooter and buzzed off in the direction of town, giving a little *toot-toot* and wave to the Auxiliary women as she passed.

Once the chains were unhooked from the coffin and the excavator was out of the way, I helped the guys guide the church truck into the back of my hearse. Before I shut the door, I had a sick feeling that someone was watching me. Of course the crowd was still there, but I mean someone was watching *my* every move.

I looked back over my shoulder toward the trailer park. The man in the John Deere hat popped behind the tree when he saw me look at him.

I shut the hearse door and got into the driver's side. Before I left the cemetery, I looked in my rearview mirror at the tree. The man was standing there. This time the shadow of the hat didn't hide his eyes.

We locked eyes.

"Look away," Chicken Teater warned me when he appeared in the passenger seat.